"Can you please just be straight with me?"

"Of course." He arched a light brown eyebrow at her. "I don't appreciate that you think the worst of me. And given the way my own father just erased me from his life, it gets under my skin that people are determined to write me off."

The accusation hit home with pinpoint accuracy.

No matter that she believed Gavin had earned his reputation, a part of her still felt the sting of his allegation.

"So, if we're going to work together on this bachelor auction, I'd appreciate it if you'd take the time to get to know me. Go on a date with me, Lauryn." That trademark smile returned at full wattage, a potent weapon in his seductive arsenal, as he lowered his voice a notch. "Find out for yourself if I'm as bad as everyone says."

* * *

Rodeo Rebel by Joanne Rock is part of the Kingsland Ranch series.

Dear Reader,

When I have a fun idea for a story, I like to explore it every which way. After seeing the Barclay sisters through an inheritance drama in my Harlequin Desire series Return to Catamount, I kept thinking about what a problematic last will and testament would do in a family of sons. Before I even finished my series of sisters, I was already deep in conversation with the men of Kingsland Ranch.

You see, these four sons of Duke Kingsley are in for a rough ride as they navigate their mercurial father's final wishes. I thought I would send women into their lives at the worst possible time, forcing them to deal with romantic feelings as they each come to terms with what their home and family really means to them. For Gavin Kingsley, that means Lauryn Hamilton, the local charity director who really needs his help—right when he needs to leave Montana for good.

I hope you'll enjoy the Kingsland Ranch series as much as I enjoyed writing it. As always, you can learn more about my upcoming books on my website, joannerock.com, including the release dates for all of the upcoming Kingsland stories!

Happy reading,

Joanne Rock

JOANNE ROCK

—

RODEO REBEL

ISBN-13: 978-1-335-58164-8

Rodeo Rebel

Copyright © 2023 by Joanne Rock

For questions and comments about the quality of this book,
please contact us at CustomerService@Harlequin.com.

Harlequin Enterprises ULC
22 Adelaide St. West, 41st Floor
Toronto, Ontario M5H 4E3, Canada
www.Harlequin.com

Printed in U.S.A.

USA TODAY bestselling author **Joanne Rock** credits her decision to write romance to a book she picked up during a flight delay that engrossed her so thoroughly, she didn't mind at all when her flight was delayed two more times. Giving her readers the chance to escape into another world has motivated her to write over one hundred books for a variety of Harlequin series.

Books by Joanne Rock

Harlequin Desire

Return to Catamount

Rocky Mountain Rivals
One Colorado Night
A Colorado Claim

Kingsland Ranch

Rodeo Rebel

Visit the Author Profile page at
Harlequin.com for more titles.

You can also find Joanne Rock on Facebook,
along with other Harlequin Desire authors,
at Facebook.com/HarlequinDesireAuthors!

Prologue

Gavin Kingsley couldn't pack his bags fast enough.

"You knew about this all along, and yet you said nothing to me." He stalked around the built-in dresser inside his spacious closet while he fumed aloud for the benefit of his oldest half brother, Levi Kingsley, currently on the other end of their teleconference.

Even now, Levi's face was framed in the tablet screen perched on a shelf between a display case of watches and the charging station for Gavin's electronics. He'd lived in this custom-built house for all of two years after agreeing to purchase land next door to the western Montana–based Kingsland Ranch, where he'd been raised. Somehow, his half brothers had convinced him to oversee the growing stud program at Kingsland, even though their father—Duke Kingsley—had never viewed Gavin as favorably as his sons by Duke's first wife.

Foolishly, Gavin had allowed himself to believe his estrangement from his father would be temporary. That Duke would welcome him back into the fold, and they'd smooth over past differences so that working together and living next door to Kingsland all made sense.

Only to be disinherited by his father's surprise will.

The memory of that moment—of the realization that he'd been an interloper in his own life, that his own father hadn't thought he deserved the Kingsley name—threatened to rip another hole through him.

Levi's voice cut through the maelstrom. "Gavin, I had no idea Dad intended to leave Kingsland Ranch solely to Quinton and me."

Not interested in his brother's explanations, Gavin swept out a drawerful of T-shirts and shoved them into a duffel bag. He'd sell the house as soon as possible. For now, he needed to catch the first flight out of Montana.

Far from Kingsland Ranch.

"I call bullshit." He yanked open a drawer of workout gear and grabbed a handful of items to add to his going-away collection of clothes. "You're a trustee of the estate. Obviously, you had to know in order to be named in the living trust—"

"Just because I'm the trustee doesn't mean I knew Dad's directives until the lawyer read them to us this afternoon," Levi shot back, his deeply olive skin showing a tinge of red as he got more fired up. He sat in his home office at the Kingsland main house, the same home where Duke had died of a heart attack two weeks before. Behind Levi, Gavin could still see the wooden sign with interlocking horseshoes that made up the ranch's logo. "The only reason he created that trust was so the estate could avoid probate and we could maintain day-to-day operations without any gap in management."

Gavin pulled out a garment bag to hold his dress shirts and suits.

"I find that tough to believe, given all the closed-door meetings you and Dad had about the trust and his plans for Kingsland." Bad enough that his brother had lied to him by omission all these years, allowing Gavin to believe he'd have part ownership of the ranch and a say in the daily operations. But his own father hadn't thought Gavin warranted a footnote in his will.

But then, Duke had long looked at Gavin as less than worthy. Duke's two sons, Levi and Quinton, had been born of a love match between Duke and Adele Boudreaux, the daughter of one of the most successful horse breeders in Texas. After Adele's sudden death in a riding accident, Duke had married for convenience's sake, turning to his housekeeper, Isla Mitchell, as a temporary nanny for the boys. Gavin's mother had never escaped the taint of that domestic situation in her wealthy husband's eyes. After their divorce five years later, Gavin continued to have privileges at the ranch, but he'd spent a considerable part of his youth attempting to gain his dad's approval. Tough to do when he hadn't lived at Kingsland full-time. He and his mother had a downgraded lifestyle, where Gavin felt more like a visitor in his father's home than a son. Later, in his bull-riding days, he'd quit striving for approval and indulged his wild side, content to stir Duke's anger in a classic case of "some attention is better than no attention." But Gavin had cleaned up his act years ago and assumed he'd be included in the family business eventually.

Hell, he'd had faith in that idea so completely he'd allowed Levi to talk him into building his home next door to the Kingsley acreage.

"Well, believe it," Levi fired back, shoving a hand through dark hair that favored his French Creole mother. "And you can't leave now when we're about to launch the stud program. We can't do this without you—"

"Excellent. I can't deny I'm pleased to hear that," Gavin retorted. "Considering the blow I've been dealt this morning—to say nothing of Dad's illegitimate son, who got screwed over even more than me—I like the idea of the new business failing spectacularly without me."

Even though he'd worked his ass off to assemble all the right pieces and the right horses to launch the Kingsland breeding program. He hadn't thought twice about pooling his resources with his brothers', assuming they would all benefit from Kingsland's success. Now he wished like hell he were launching the stud services under his own ranch's name. He needed to consult a lawyer to figure out how to untwine his finances from his family's.

"Gav, the kickoff event is just a few weeks away. And we already promised Lauryn Hamilton that Kingsland would sponsor the bachelor auction to benefit her horse rescue since the timing coincides with our launch." Levi leveled a scowl at him. "Do you mean to tell me you're going to let her down after all the hoops she jumped through to pitch this thing to us?"

Gavin's hand paused on the zipper of the garment bag as he envisioned Lauryn's disappointed—gorgeous—face if the Kingsley family backed out of the fundraiser she'd worked tirelessly to pull together. He'd been the point person for Kingsland and had even promised her he'd go onstage to offer himself as a bachelor.

Something he wouldn't have done for anyone but her, a woman who'd intrigued him for years yet had previously kept him at arm's length because of the reputation he'd earned during those hell-raising days of his bull-riding career.

Part of that may have been because Gavin had run afoul of her adoptive father, who also happened to be the local sheriff. There'd been a long-standing enmity between him and Sheriff Hamilton after Gavin had torn through his newly planted cornfield on four-wheelers at midnight with some buddies when he'd been all of fifteen. Clearly, the man didn't believe in character redemption, even though Gavin had personally replanted the field. The sheriff had continued to hound him for the slightest misstep for years.

But her dad might not have been the only reason for the distance Lauryn kept between them. After college, she'd spent two years in Duke Kingsley's employ, working as his administrative assistant while she saved money to start her horse rescue since she was a passionate champion of providing homes for animals that had been neglected or abandoned.

Lauryn's rescue, Hooves and Hearts, now operated just a few miles down the road from Kingsland in the small town of Silent Spring, Montana. But given that she'd worked closely with Gavin's father for two years, he had to wonder if part of her refusal to give him the time of day—apart from this new fundraiser, Studs for Sale—was because Duke's view of Gavin had further tainted her own.

Making him wonder…as Duke's administrative assistant, had Lauryn been privy to the will that left Gavin with nothing?

Gritting his teeth, he shouldered the duffel bag and tried to collect himself before answering more calmly. "It's not me who let Lauryn down. If the event doesn't happen, it's your father's doing, not mine."

If it had been just a matter of money, Gavin wouldn't have even cared. He could make his own fortune, Kingsley wealth be damned.

But he'd been denied the ranch. His home. His livelihood. Something he'd assumed was his birthright as a Kingsley. A fresh wave of fury threatened to drag him under again, and he had to shake himself to ward off the anger.

Levi launched into another argument, but Gavin switched off the device to end the connection. He was too angry to field questions about his decisions right now. The hurt was too raw. The resentment all-consuming. His dad hadn't even bothered to explain the omission of his other sons in the will. Gavin and Clayton Reynolds—a son by a mistress—hadn't warranted even that much.

Gavin needed some time to get his head around what had happened so he could forge a new course for himself. One that didn't have anything to do with Kingsland Ranch.

Rationally, he knew he would miss working with Quinton and Levi. It hadn't been their fault Gavin had been disinherited. And he would miss their help with the stud program he'd taken so much pride in developing.

But he wasn't about to just hand over all his hard work to his brothers now. The breeding business couldn't launch with the Kingsland name on it—not when Gavin was no longer in the Kingsley fold. They'd need to draw up a division of assets.

A divorce from his own family.

Yet—as he stalked through the living area of the massive home he'd built to overlook the Madison River, which snaked past Kingsland's grazing pastures and created a boundary between his holding and his family's—Gavin was surprised to realize that despite all the hell that had rained down on his head today, his thoughts still circled around the fact that he'd have to disappoint Lauryn Hamilton. But not even the lure of her mysterious hazel eyes or her deep, throaty laugh that always sounded like she was thinking something slightly wicked could make him stay where his contributions weren't acknowledged or appreciated.

He'd kept Lauryn safely in his personal fantasies for years. For now, she'd just have to stay there since the last thing he needed was any attachment to this godforsaken place.

One

Fit to be tied, Lauryn Hamilton steered her pickup truck along the Madison River, past the well-known Montana ranch where she'd worked for two years. But Kingsland, with its interlocking-horseshoes logo and endless acreage, wasn't her destination today.

The road was paved and smooth, making it impossible to kick up a cloud of dust and gravel the way she would have preferred as she drove toward the man who had stood her up this afternoon. Because this level of anger required some kind of physical outlet. If not dust clouds and gravel, then throwing her meeting notes in Gavin Kingsley's face would have to suffice.

She stomped harder on the accelerator, beyond ready to confront the charismatic bad boy of Silent Spring. He'd made a big deal about chasing her for years—

behaving as though he wanted her even as he gladly
dated every woman in her age bracket for miles around.
Then, the one time when she'd actually needed the flirtatious rancher to show up for her—to help her get the
Studs for Sale event off the ground—he hadn't bothered to put in an appearance.

Even though he'd chosen the time and date for the
planning meeting weeks ago. He'd agreed to sponsor
the auction that would be held at Kingsland Ranch. Had
even seemed excited about it. Didn't he have any sense
of responsibility?

The main ranch house came into view a moment later,
but Lauryn bypassed the mammoth two-story family
compound to seek out Gavin's place. She'd never visited
it personally, but she'd heard all about the home's con-
struction two years ago since the former bull rider had
always been a subject for gossip among Silent Spring
locals. His good looks and bad boy reputation had made
it impossible to avoid talk of his escapades ever since
she'd moved here, back when her parents had adopted
her at twelve years old after the most traumatic month
of her life.

Rubbing a hand over one shoulder where the scars
of that time had left her with a visible reminder of old
hurts, Lauryn could still recall hearing about Gavin for
the first time, when he'd driven through her dad's fields
at midnight. At first, she'd envisioned a boy similar to
her—someone in a foster home, who'd had a rough
start to life—when she'd imagined what the late-night
intruder might be like. When she'd learned that he was

the son of the wealthiest man in town, an overindulged Kingsley son, her curiosity about him had vanished.

They'd always been worlds apart, from their very different beginnings to the way Gavin thumbed his nose at the world while she strove to make people like her. But when Gavin had agreed to help her with the Studs for Sale event, she'd believed—briefly—that he'd changed.

The more fool her.

Moments later, the newly constructed cedar home came into view. Smaller than the main residence but impressive nevertheless, the two-story building was L-shaped around a wide redbrick driveway with darker pavers laid out in the pattern of the Kingsland horseshoe logo. Lauryn parked her truck right in the middle of the emblem and jumped down to the ground, her boots striking the stone pavers with determined steps.

Checking her watch, she noted the time was half past noon before she stepped onto the porch and raised her fist to knock on the door.

"Gavin." She called his name as she rapped quickly on the wooden barrier. "It's Lauryn. I need to speak with you."

No answer came.

Not by word or deed. The door remained shut, the house remained quiet and her call went unanswered.

Where could he be? He knew how important the Studs for Sale event was to her. Her horse rescue desperately needed the infusion of capital the bachelor auction would bring since she was expanding the rescue into an equine-therapy program—an effort close to her heart, considering how much it had helped her recover from the trauma she'd experienced as a child.

Knowing that Hooves and Hearts would benefit from the auction, she'd done all the preplanning work herself to make certain that her sponsors could make a difference simply by writing a check. But Gavin had wanted to take on a bigger role since her event coincided with the launch of Kingsland's breeding service. Her Studs for Sale bachelor auction would naturally bring a lot of spotlight to Kingsland. It made no sense for Gavin to abandon the project now.

Peering around the quiet front courtyard, she spied empty wooden benches beside manicured dwarf trees, chokecherry bushes full of white blooms and pink bitterroot flowers climbing over low rocks. Everything well tended.

But no Gavin. She'd already left two disgruntled messages for him, so she didn't see any point in calling again.

Lifting her phone, she opened the screen this time to text Quinton, Gavin's brother, who'd agreed to be one of the bachelors auctioned off for Studs for Sale. His tech business had brought him a different kind of visibility than his siblings and—she hoped—his fame in the digital community would attract all the more attendees to the auction.

But her big draw remained Gavin. His bull-riding fame had brought him a huge following that would welcome the opportunity to bid on an evening with him. She walked over to one of the benches near the chokecherry bush and took a seat in the spring sunlight to type.

Do you know where Gavin is? He missed a meeting on
the bachelor auction.

She glanced up from the phone, still hoping to see
some sign of Gavin. Returning from the fields on a tractor, maybe. Or riding up on horseback. But the only sound
in the stillness was her phone chiming with an incoming text.

Haven't heard from him since he took off after our father's will reading. The old man cut Gavin out of everything.

The statement took her a moment to absorb. Lauryn knew Duke Kingsley had died two weeks prior.
She'd once worked for the man, but they'd never been
close. To show her respects, she had attended the wake
with her mom and had offered condolences to the three
Kingsley sons who'd attended. But she hadn't heard
anything about the family patriarch's will.

Gavin "took off"? Her stomach knotted at what that
might mean for her event.

Her fingers hovered over her phone since she had no
idea how to respond. Before she could decide, another
text from Quinton appeared.

Not sure about Kingsland sponsoring the bachelor auction now, Lauryn, since we can't run the breeding business without Gav. But you're still welcome to hold the
event at Kingsland.

Things went from bad to worse. The gala was just three weeks away. She thanked Quinton for the information and told him she'd get back to him about the auction.

Distress over the event and her frustration with Gavin were certainly tempered by the news that he'd been cut out of his father's will completely. He must be devastated. And no matter how much Gavin had gotten under her skin over the years, she hated to think of his dad pulling the rug out from under him that way.

She walked toward her pickup truck as she debated her options, ducking away from a honeybee buzzing nearby. And in the quiet that followed, just as she reached for the door handle of her vehicle, she heard the rumble of an engine in the distance.

A sound that grew louder, as if coming closer.

The ranch road wound past Gavin's house and continued on to the lower pastures. Conceivably, a ranch hand could be driving out to work on fences or check on animals in those fields.

Yet some sense tickled the back of her neck like a premonition.

A sense confirmed a moment later when a familiar oversize black pickup came into view.

Gavin's truck.

Her heart pounded faster as he drove closer, the outline of his face becoming visible as he neared. Stetson in place, he locked eyes with her through the windshield, his brown gaze like a laser beam as he held her in his sights.

Inexplicably, her pulse stuttered and then quickened.

The black sheep of Kingsland Ranch had returned.

* * *

So much for returning to Silent Spring without anyone noticing.

Gavin met the challenging hazel gaze of the town's sexiest woman as he drove toward his house. Lauryn Hamilton stood in the middle of his driveway, arms crossed, chin tilted up. She was dressed for business in a figure-hugging short-sleeved navy blue dress that buttoned all the way up the front, the hem brushing the tops of her high-heeled chocolate brown boots. Long chestnut-colored waves rested on her shoulders, her full lips pursed in a moue of displeasure.

Today hadn't been the first time he'd seen that expression on her face when she looked his way, so it shouldn't bug him so much now. Especially when that pout of hers was so sexy it ought to be NSFW. But Gavin couldn't enjoy the sight of those plump pink lips quite as much now, knowing he was only going to disappoint her further when he told her he was backing out of the bachelor auction.

Behind him on the jump seat, the thump, thump, thump of his Rottweiler's tail reminded Gavin that he wasn't the only one who'd spotted their guest.

"Maybe you can put a smile on her face, Rocco. I've got my work cut out for me otherwise," he observed as he parked his truck alongside hers. "I could use the backup."

Gavin cracked open the door and stepped down to the brick driveway before opening the rear cab door and unhooking the carabiner from the pup's harness. While Rocco bounded out of the truck, Gavin pasted on a polite smile, having learned from past experience that behavior trending toward charming or flirtatious would only earn scorn from the horse-rescue owner.

"Hello, Lauryn. To what do I owe the pleasure?" He reached in to remove an empty trunk from the cargo bed while Rocco approached Lauryn with a butt-wiggling tail wag.

At least Rocco was able to get some love from her. Lauryn scratched behind his ears, assuring the Rottweiler-husky mix that he was a very good boy.

A sentiment he guessed she wouldn't be sharing with him.

While Rocco soaked up the attention, Gavin slid the trunk onto the driveway, well aware of his mission to pack up more clothes while he figured out his next move.

Seven days on a beach in Mexico—some more sober than others—hadn't been enough to help him cool off about being disinherited. But now that he'd mourned the loss of the life he'd thought he was going to lead, he was ready to make a new plan that didn't include the Kingsleys.

"The pleasure?" Straightening from where she'd been petting the dog, Lauryn followed him toward the house as he carried his trunk to the front porch while Rocco trotted off to the barns. "It is not a pleasure for me, Gavin, because I wasted the whole morning waiting around for you to begin a planning meeting for the bachelor auction. Needless to say, you never showed up."

Ah, damn.

He paused in the middle of entering his security code for the front door, regret slamming him for the oversight.

"Was that today? I should have messaged you." He'd thought about it a few times during his week of drinking away the past, his father and all the hopes he'd had for a life in Montana working beside his brothers. But whenever a thought of the Studs for Sale event crossed his mind, urging him to call Lauryn, he either hadn't had his phone handy, hadn't been able to get good reception or had ended up thinking about Lauryn in ways that weren't at all businesslike…

"I would have appreciated a heads-up," she agreed, stopping at the edge of his porch as if there was an invisible line there she wouldn't follow him across. "Better yet, you could have been there with us since Kingsland is the biggest sponsor. I specifically arranged the best time for you so you could ensure the event showcased the ranch." Her tone stopped short of being chastising, no doubt because of the clout and capital at stake while she believed him to represent Kingsland's interests.

How fast would that change once she found out he was backing out of the event?

He knew she'd always been wary around him. That her father's opinions of him—and her own dad's familiarity with the scrapes he'd gotten into as a younger man—had colored her view of him. Her cool demeanor ever since she'd arrived in Silent Spring as the sheriff's adopted daughter had told Gavin that she didn't think much of him. But in their two previous meetings about

Studs for Sale, he'd had reason to believe maybe he was changing her mind about him.

Not that he needed her good opinion, damn it.

His head pounded with the stress of coming up with a solution on the fly. He should have been thinking about this kind of thing for the last week, but simply getting through the days with the knowledge that his own father had thought him unworthy of the family legacy had been hellish.

Stabbing the rest of the code into the buttons on the security pad, Gavin disarmed the system and opened the door to settle his trunk in the foyer. Then he stepped outside again to finish their conversation.

"I'm sorry, Lauryn." Restless and edgy about a topic he didn't want to have with anyone, let alone a woman whose view of him had always been biased, he rocked back on his heels while he measured his words. "I've been reeling this week since learning my father cut me out of Kingsland Ranch in his will."

He studied her reaction carefully, searching for the slightest hint that she'd had previous intelligence of his father's intentions during the years she'd been Duke's assistant.

And, lo and behold, a nervous swipe of her tongue along her upper lip was her only visible response. She didn't seem surprised by the news. Only…uneasy?

His suspicion about her connection to his father grew. Not just because she might know more than she was saying. But also because she could have tainted his father's opinion of him.

"It's my turn to apologize, Gavin." Her gaze flicked to the ground, where she shifted her feet before meeting his again. She shaded her eyes to look at him in the strong afternoon sunlight, her tone softening. "I heard the news about the will from Quinton when I called him a little while ago, and I can't imagine how upsetting the last few weeks have been since your dad's passing."

A conversation with his brother would explain why the news about being disinherited hadn't surprised her. Yet her cool composure still gave him misgivings about how much she knew and when she'd learned of it. Sun beating down on his shoulders, he pointed toward the shaded area at the end of the house and gestured for her to follow him as he answered.

"'Upsetting' would be an understatement. More like someone cut me off at the knees." Hating the way that could be construed as self-pitying, he halted just inside the shaded overhang with a view of the Madison River. Pivoting to face her, he cut to the chase. "That's why today's meeting completely slipped my mind. I've been thinking about next steps, and all that really remains clear to me right now is I can't stay here."

Lauryn had been following close behind him, but she took a step back now, grazing a rocking chair with her knee. She reached long, manicured fingers blindly out to one side to steady herself on the back of the chair.

"What do you mean? You can't stay at the house any-more?" Her dark eyebrows knit in confusion. "Quinton mentioned you've been gone—"

"As in, I can't live in a house next to Kingsland any-more. I don't even plan to stay in Montana. And unfortunately, I won't be able to represent Kingsland at the bachelor auction, so I'm not going to participate."

At her gasp, he hastened to add, "I'll donation match, of course. Just let me know what you think an average bid for a bachelor might have been, and I'll write a check."

Two

Heaven help her.

Even after being disinherited, Gavin Kingsley assumed he could fix every problem by writing a check.

As if he hadn't just swung a sledgehammer through an event she'd spent months preparing.

Lauryn stared at him as he tugged off his Stetson and set it on the patio table nearby, his faded jeans hugging lean hips while he turned. An olive green Henley shirt showcased his strong arms and shoulders, his build taller than many of the most successful bull riders. And yet he'd made a name for himself in the years he'd competed, earning prizes and recognition that even his cynical father had grudgingly noticed. Not that he'd been impressed. Duke Kingsley had told Lauryn that Gavin only sought out the rodeo to avoid real work.

A sentiment her dad would have surely echoed if she'd ever asked his opinion. Certainly her father had weighed in enough times in the past weeks about her decision to approach Gavin to do the bachelor auction in the first place. Logically, she understood that Sheriff Caleb Hamilton couldn't help but view the black sheep Kingsley with a jaundiced eye. Silent Spring's local lawman had had plenty of opportunities to field phone calls when a younger Gavin would slip into local pastures to practice bull riding on the neighboring ranches' rankest bulls. Or when he'd organize drag races near the river on summer weekends, risking his neck to push a car as hard as it could go.

Or so she'd heard.

She had friends who'd attended those races and spoke with breathless admiration about Gavin's daring and control as he beat out the field with his prowess behind the wheel. Yet she'd never actually attended one of those underground meets.

But it had been years since he'd done things like that. A change tracked roughly to when he'd quit the pro bull-riding circuit so he could help his brothers with Kingsland. Lauryn had been too busy starting up her equine rescue at the time to take much notice of his return to town, but he'd certainly turned the heads of all her friends. And while he'd maintained his devil-may-care approach to dating, his work ethic had seemed admirable. Up until today's missed meeting, in fact, Lauryn had been impressed by his commitment to her fundraiser event. He hadn't tried to lay on the charm with her or make sly remarks when she'd suggested the Studs for Sale name.

If anything, he'd been readily supportive of the rescue, offering suggestions to make the evening flow smoothly and connecting her with two other eligible bachelors who promised to excite lots of bidding.

She'd thought that he'd turned a corner from his old ways.

But today, he'd stood her up at an important meeting and offered to buy his way out of a commitment.

Now Gavin ran a hand through his longish brown hair, tucking a few shorter strands behind his ear. The stubble around his jaw and mouth was several days past shaving, the effect only adding to his rugged sex appeal.

Or it would be, if she were a woman who sought out bad boys, which she most decidedly was not. Gavin Kingsley might be going through a truly rough time in his life right now, but that didn't mean she would let down her guard around a man who—for most of his life—had played fast and loose with rules.

And women.

The reminder made her stuff down the urge to console him. To tell him she understood how losing a parent could make someone feel adrift and alone.

"Gavin." His name sounded too intimate on her lips. Was it because of the thoughts she'd been having about him? She dragged in a breath scented with heather and catmint from the flower bed surrounding the patio. "I'm grateful for the offer of a donation, but what this event really needs is *you*. Your contacts, your participation."

"You mean *Kingsley* contacts." His lip curled. But then his dog trotted toward them again, the black face with tan points appearing suddenly from behind a thicket near the river's edge, and Gavin's expression eased. He whistled for his pet, causing the Rottweiler mix to kick it into a higher gear as he headed toward the porch. "Maybe Levi or Quinton will—"

"No, I need *you*." She said it with emphasis, and as soon as the words were out there, she heard how personal that sounded. Her cheeks warmed, and she was glad for a reason to turn her face away from Gavin as Rocco reached them. She scratched the dog's ears, having gotten to know the handsome Rotty well during the years she worked for Duke since Gavin had visited the main house frequently. "That is, you bring something different to the table than your brothers. You're…" She struggled to find a tactful way to say that women from halfway across the state had told Lauryn they were attending the event to bid on a date with the sought-after bachelor rancher. "…very popular."

"So I'll find someone to take my place." He raised his arms in exasperation, making Rocco whine a sympathetic chorus even as the dog left Lauryn to sit beside his owner. "Lauryn, I can't be a part of this. I'm done with Kingsland for good."

Anxiety balled in her gut as she realized how serious he was about this. Could he really bail on her this late in the game?

His face was on the event website. A popular internet blog devoted to cowgirl life had planned a feature. Two national horse publications were covering the fundraiser, a fact that had appealed to Gavin when the launch of Kingsland's stud program was set to coincide with the bachelor auction.

"So participate under your own ranch name. Don't go as Kingsland. Go to represent Broken Spur." She pointed to the wooden sign on the vintage silo close to the river.

Unlike the sleekly stylized horseshoes logo of Kingsland, the Broken Spur sign used an actual rusty spur sticking out of the wooden placard at an awkward angle.

"Seriously? I didn't even pick the name. I just inherited it when I bought the place." Bending to scoop up a rope chew toy that lay nearby, Gavin waved it in front of Rocco before winging it out onto lawn, sending the dog running. "It's not like I'm planning to do business here—"

"So you're going to just hand over the stud program to your brothers?" She'd edged closer to make her point.

Pushing at his pride.

Pushing her agenda because her rescue deserved her best efforts. She'd invested too much time with Studs for Sale to let the event fall short of all it could accomplish. She recalled with perfect clarity the moment a piece of her soul had begun to heal because of equine therapy. She owed her ability to move forward in life to horses, and she planned to pay that gift forward to other people wandering the world, feeling hollow inside.

"Hell no." Emotion flashed in his brown eyes when he turned her way. Anger. Resentment. "But I don't have a plan yet to launch the business when I need to untwine my financial interests from theirs."

They stood entirely too near. Breathing each other's air in a silent moment that stretched out between them.

The musk and leather scent of him made her want to step closer still. Then his gaze flicked lower, raking over her mouth. Lingering. A shiver rolled through her, skin prickling with awareness. But then, reminding herself who she was talking to and how much she didn't want to be just another woman who fell under his spell, Lauryn edged back again.

"What will it take to make you reconsider?" Needing some space between them, a distraction from the pull he exerted over her, Lauryn bent to take the chew toy Rocco had proudly returned to them.

When she flung it as far onto the lawn as possible, she could feel Gavin's eyes on her.

"My presence is that important to you?" The timbre of his voice, smoky and soft, tripped up her spine in a peculiar way.

She shook off the sensation, admonishing herself that this talk had to be all business.

Hooves and Hearts needed the income from this event too much for her to get caught up in whatever games Gavin liked to play with women.

Games she suspected he excelled at.

"The invitations have gone out," she explained, chasing the image of sensual playtime from her brain. Where had that come from? She wished his conscience would just kick in and explain to him that a responsible adult would make good on his word to be a part of the fundraiser. "Guests have RSVP'd. They all think you're going to be there."

His jaw worked, flexing and tensing, as he seemed to chew over the idea. Once more, his attention dipped lower, taking her in from boots to breasts.

Or maybe her breasts just noticed his attention more

than the rest of her. Her face flamed hot, and she found herself sliding one hand beneath her hair to lift the mass that felt too warm against her neck.

Catching herself in the act, she released it once more, yanking her arms to her side as she realized his gaze was calmly fixed on her face again, his expression masked.

"If I do this for you, I wouldn't be going for the sake of the guests." Something about his words made her wary even as hope reignited.

"Meaning you might attend after all?" She searched his brown eyes, looking for the catch.

"On one condition." His chin ticked up.

She sensed a challenge coming, but she needed his participation too much to care.

"Name it."

Between them, Rocco's furry body brushed against her, the dog's panting audible as he waited for another round of fetch. But she didn't dare look away from Gavin as she mentally urged him to follow through with the auction.

As if she could impose her will on him if she stared hard enough.

"Go on a date with me."

He couldn't have surprised her more if he'd asked her to drag race him.

In the silence that ensued, she heard a tractor at work in the distance, a sign of the Broken Spur's fields being worked nearby. The engine hummed in chorus with the warning bells jangling in her brain.

"Excuse me?" She'd heard him clearly enough. But

she had to be missing something since he'd never made an overture toward her.

She'd assumed the occasional hot looks that he sent her way were a knee-jerk reaction, an automatic facet of being a ladies' man. They'd had little to do with her personally.

No doubt he flirted with everyone that way.

"It's a simple request, Lauryn. I'd like—just once—to take you on a date." Never looking away from her, he gave a soothing scratch to Rocco's head and somehow released the dog from the game with some kind of nonverbal command.

Or so she guessed since Rocco took his toy onto a rug near the back door, where he lay down and put his head between his paws with a long doggy huff.

Rocco seemed to comprehend the man in front of her far better than she ever would.

"I don't understand. Why would you want to do that?" She already knew she would agree. Of course she would say yes for the good of the charity event.

The man was a sought-after bachelor for a reason, not the least of which were his good looks and magnetic charm. Women threw themselves at him. And while he'd always moved on quickly from them, Lauryn had never heard any complaints other than that they were sad when their time with him came to an end.

There was an implied compliment in that.

But she wanted to know why Gavin would request such a thing when he could have dozens of women lining up to be his very willing partner for any given night.

A ghost of his old, careless grin crossed his face.

"No need to sound so surprised." He leaned a square shoulder against the wooden post at the edge of the patio, as if settling in for a casual conversation when his words had thrown her into a whirlwind of confused anxiety. "I don't think you need for me to tell you you're a very compelling woman."

Flustered, she shook her head.

"Don't be ridiculous. I'm not fishing for compliments, Gavin. I just can't fathom how a date with me will make it any more bearable for you to participate in an event you're obviously now dreading." An awful thought occurred to her. "Is this about my father? A way to tick off the sheriff?"

Any hint of a smile vanished.

"How little you think of me," he observed wryly, shaking his head. "Although, oddly enough, even as you offend me, you manage to tap into a reason that I want this date."

Impatience stiffened her spine. Tension tightened in her shoulders.

"You're talking in riddles. Can you please just be straight with me?"

"Of course." He arched a light brown eyebrow at her, as if she were the one playing word games. "I don't appreciate that you think the worst of me. And given the way my own father just erased me from his life, it gets under my skin that people are determined to write me off."

The accusation hit home with pinpoint accuracy.

No matter that she believed Gavin had well-earned

his reputation, a part of her still felt the sting of his allegation. She pursed her lips, unsure how to respond.

But he saved her from replying when he continued speaking a moment later, "So, if we're going to work together on this bachelor auction, I'd appreciate it if you'd take the time to get to know me. Go on a date with me, Lauryn." That trademark smile returned at full wattage, a potent weapon in his seductive arsenal, as he lowered his voice a notch. "Find out for yourself if I'm as bad as everyone says."

Three

Gavin knew Lauryn wouldn't refuse.

Yet having the ice queen of Silent Spring over a barrel didn't give him the satisfaction it might have at one time. Maybe because he had every reason to suspect she'd played a role in depriving him of the family legacy, a concern that left him feeling more bitter than vengeful since he couldn't do anything to change the fact that Duke Kingsley had gone to his grave assuming the worst of his son.

"Fine. It's a deal." Lauryn thrust her hand toward him to seal the bargain. "One date in exchange for your participation in the bachelor auction—both as a bachelor and as a sponsor."

He noted she was careful to spell that out.

Smart businesswoman.

And yet the gesture provided all the more proof that she thought him less than honorable. Making him doubly glad he'd come up with the date scheme as a way to learn more about her and how much she'd known about his disinheritance.

"We're in agreement," he assured her, taking her soft, slender fingers in his to seal the deal.

Beneath his thumb, in the tender vee of her palm, he felt the warm throb of her pulse beneath her skin. A rhythmic beat that jumped faster when he gave it a small, tentative stroke.

For a moment, Lauryn's hazel gaze flashed with startled awareness.

Right before she drew her hand free.

"Then let's agree to a time to go over the meeting notes I had ready for this morning," she murmured, folding her arms across her chest in a way that made her breasts all the more enticing.

Not that he let his gaze linger.

He wasn't about to push a seduction agenda with a woman whose good will he required if he was going to draw her out about her relationship with his father. Although somewhere along the way, he wouldn't mind hearing Lauryn Hamilton acknowledge that the chemistry between them wasn't all one sided.

"How about the day after tomorrow?" He'd need to rearrange his schedule since he'd already agreed to meet a Realtor the next day to view ranch properties in Wyoming.

Now Gavin would need to cool his heels in Montana for at least a few more weeks until the bachelor auction.

"It will have to be after noon," she answered without even consulting a schedule. "I'm driving out to Twin Bridges that morning to deliver a four-year-old mare to a family who fell in love with her after visiting the rescue last month."

The warmth in her voice, the glow in her face at the mention of the animals in her care, told everything about her commitment to her cause. No matter what Gavin learned about his father from her—or not—he could hardly begrudge the time and investment in someone so dedicated to equine rescue.

"That's fine," he assured her, gesturing toward the walkway back toward the front of the house where her pickup waited beside his so he could escort her out. He had new plans to make for his remaining days in Silent Spring. "If you're running late that day, just shoot me a text. I can meet later, if necessary."

As they moved out of the covered-patio area, Rocco rose to follow, tail wagging sleepily after his doze. To keep his attention off the enticing sway of Lauryn's hips as they walked, Gavin allowed his attention to move to the custom-built ranch house he'd spent so long designing to his exact specifications—from the detached garage with separate kitchen and suite for guests to the hand-hewn timber used in the living area and the spectacular river views. He would miss the place when he left, but this work with Lauryn would keep him here a little while longer.

"Thank you." Lauryn shifted her hair to the opposite shoulder as they walked, a few silky waves brushing his arm. "But I don't anticipate any problems.

The adopter is an experienced horseman buying the mare for his teenage daughter. I know he's got the stable and pasture ready, and he's paid in advance for a year's worth of hay."

"Sounds like your ideal customer," Gavin observed as they reached her truck. "Where would you like to meet?"

She nibbled her lip as she thought, and Gavin distracted himself from her mouth by reaching for the handle on the driver's-side door.

"Would you mind if we worked here? Your place is on the way back from Twin Bridges."

The thought of having her all to himself again sent a surge of red-hot desire through him. He tried to ignore it, grateful he'd have a couple of days to come up with a plan for their time together.

Because he would swear that the chemistry between them had grown more potent this afternoon. While he'd always felt the draw just beneath the surface of their interactions, he'd seen a hint of her reaction to him today, and that had amped up the heat far beyond anything the mild spring sun dished out.

"Of course. And if you send me the meeting notes ahead of time, I'll be all the more prepared." He made the offer mostly so he could devote more of their time together to conversation about her. He needed to find casual ways to get her talking about those years in his father's employment.

Yet to see the obvious pleasure she took in the gesture, he almost felt guilty for the ulterior motive.

"That would be fantastic." Her eyes lit up as she

looked at him. "I'll shoot them your way once I get home."

Holding the door for her while she stepped up on the running board of her sporty red pickup truck, Gavin couldn't help but see a flash of her bare legs as her navy sheath dress hiked up away from the tops of her suede boots.

Rocco chose that moment to bark, looking back and forth between them.

A friendly goodbye to their guest? Or a reminder to Gavin to put his eyes back in his head?

He gritted his teeth, guessing it was the latter, while Lauryn's gaze shifted to the dog before she laughed with pleasure.

"It was good to see you, too, Rocco," she said sweetly, reaching down to scratch the dog's head before she tucked her dress more securely around her legs. "I'll be back at the Broken Spur before you know it."

Gavin told himself it was stupid to envy his pet, but the big fur-beast was damned lucky to have Lauryn's long fingers stroke him. No wonder the tail-wagging recommenced with renewed enthusiasm.

"See you then," Gavin managed over a dry throat as he shut the door behind her.

Stepping back with a wave, he watched her pull out of the driveway.

And no matter that he'd gotten out of the meeting exactly what he wanted—an opportunity to find out how much Lauryn had known about his father's plans to disinherit him and what role she might have played in the decision—Gavin couldn't help but think he'd signed on for a whole lot more than he bargained for.

Two days later, Lauryn folded her arms on the four-rail fence behind her client's spacious home in Twin Bridges.

In the pasture in front of her, she watched Toffee, the bay mare, explore her new surroundings. The horse nosed a pile of clean straw behind her brand-new stable, then walked slowly toward a black spruce tree that would provide good shade in the summer.

"She seems right at home, doesn't she?" a familiar feminine voice said behind her.

Turning, Lauryn met the kind eyes of her former foster mother, Ellen Crawford. The older woman looked exactly the same as Lauryn remembered her from her brief stay with the Crawfords before the Hamiltons adopted her when she was twelve years old. Maybe a few strands of the blond ponytail that hung over the shoulder of her red flannel shirt were grayer, but the keen blue eyes were just as warm, the walk just as full of vigor. Ellen and her husband, Chip, had fostered children right up until a few months ago, when they adopted their last foster daughter, Zara, now the lucky recipient of the bay mare they'd taken in from Lauryn's rescue.

"Toffee is going to love this place." Opening her arms for a hug, Lauryn gave the tall, spare woman a quick squeeze, the earthy scent of herbs clinging to her from her work in the greenhouse next door, where the Crawfords sold plants and trees. "But then, you have a knack for making everyone feel at home here."

Ellen smiled her pleasure as she joined Lauryn at
the rail. "She'll be good company for Zara. I remember how horses helped you come back to life after you
moved here."

Memories crowded her thoughts, the sudden in-
trusion of the past uncomfortable, even though she'd
worked through the worst of it a long time ago. Ellen
Crawford was the only person in Lauryn's life who
could speak so openly about the horror she'd faced in
her previous foster home.

Not that she'd been mistreated. Her then-family had
been kind enough, if a little overwhelmed by the number of children under their roof at the time. Their home
had been an aging farmhouse, and there'd been plenty
of room for them all and fun places to explore. An attic.
A basement. Barns and outbuildings. Much of it hadn't
been in use at the time, but Lauryn and her favorite foster
sister, thirteen-year-old Jamie, hadn't heeded their parents' warnings about staying out of the older structures.
They'd grown comfortable in their "hideouts," sneaking
books into their best-loved haunts to escape chores or
avoid their brothers.

Not that they needed a reason. Both had been caught
up in the joys of having a real sister and best friend, a
first for each of them. They'd been glad just to spend
time together, sharing every secret while they braided
one another's hair and dreamed of living next door to
each other once they were old enough to leave the foster home.

A dream that had never happened for Jamie.

After the accident, Lauryn didn't recall much until

she'd arrived at the Crawfords' home and her new foster mom, Ellen, introduced her to equine therapy. Over the next several months, Lauryn found a new best friend in the understanding brown eyes of a Champagne quarter horse gelding.

"Champy was a godsend," Lauryn admitted, her voice thick with the memory of the bond they'd formed. A downside of her adoption by the Hamiltons had been their insistence that she not visit her quarter horse friend anymore—or anyone from her past—believing a fresh start would be best. She hadn't complained about it, sensing that, as a twelve-year-old with a traumatic history, she'd been fortunate to find a forever family at all.

"I'd forgotten his name." Ellen chuckled softly in her easy way as they watched Toffee snuffle around the black spruce needles before snorting in disapproval at the scent and backing away. "Champy. What a good horse."

For a moment, they remembered the gelding in companionable silence. That ability to sit with uncomfortable things—sadness, memories—was one of the reasons Lauryn had sought Ellen out after college. As much as Lauryn adored her adoptive parents, they'd had a tough time talking about the past, and they certainly hadn't wanted her to either. No one in Silent Spring knew her real personal story because the Hamiltons had told their friends they were adopting a relative's child.

Lauryn's past had been swept under a rug.

But Jamie—like Champy—deserved remembering.

A moment later, Ellen's voice called her back to the

present. "We received your invitation to Studs for Sale. It sounds like quite the event you've put together."

Nearby, Chip stepped out of the stable and into the pasture, giving them a wave as he walked toward Toffee, brandishing an apple.

Lauryn was grateful for the extra moment to gather her thoughts about the auction. Her planning meeting with Gavin was only an hour away, and visions of seeing him again had occupied far too much space in her mind the last two days.

"I hope so. It's been a lot of work, but it will be worth it if it raises enough money to take my plans for the equine-therapy facility to the next level." She'd dreamed of this for years.

She would have never guessed what a big role Gavin would play in bringing the equine-therapy center to life.

"I was surprised to see Gavin Kingsley on the list of available bachelors." Ellen's tone was teasing as she slanted a sly look Lauryn's way. "I thought he was the last man in Silent Spring you wanted anything to do with."

"Have I said that before?" Straightening from the fence, Lauryn picked at a string from around the button of her flannel work shirt.

It sounded like something she'd thought, certainly, but she couldn't recall venting about Gavin to Ellen.

"Long ago, when you first went to work for Duke Kingsley," Ellen reminded her more gently. "I remarked that it was a job with good contacts, considering that even then you hoped to work with horses. But you made it clear Gavin was not anyone you thought very highly of."

That she'd spouted off so openly about him gave her

a little more understanding into why Gavin had insisted she get to know him.

"There's a chance I rushed to judgment about him when I was younger," she admitted, pulling back her shoulders. If she wanted people to bid on Silent Spring's resident bad boy, she shouldn't speak negatively about him, of course. That didn't mean she'd changed her opinion. "He might have more redeeming qualities than I realized now that he's an adult."

Ellen nodded as she escorted Lauryn toward the truck and horse trailer backed partially on the lawn. Chip had wanted her to unload Toffee as close to the pasture as possible in case she was spooked by the new surroundings.

"The sheriff definitely doesn't think so." Withdrawing a pair of work gloves from the back pocket of her jeans, Ellen smoothed out the crumpled fingers before putting them on, her brow furrowed. "I remember blowing by Gavin's truck one day last year when I was in a rush to get to an appointment. Then, in the rearview mirror, I saw your dad tear out from a speed trap to pull Gavin over."

The story made Lauryn a little uneasy since she'd heard from friends that her father had it "in" for Gavin. But then, Lauryn had the advantage of knowing her dad's side of things. All the old pranks. All the history.

"They definitely don't get along," she acknowledged, hoping they would be civil at the Studs for Sale event. She felt sure her parents would attend to support her, although she hadn't received their RSVP yet.

"The funny part is, Gavin hadn't been speeding. I

felt so guilty, I even called the police station to let them know they must have caught the wrong vehicle on radar and it had been *me* driving hell for leather through there. But your dad was adamant he had a reason for pulling over Gavin."

Defensiveness for her father rose.

"And I'm sure he did." She attempted to say it with levity, but the comment fell flat as she met Ellen's troubled blue gaze.

In the awkward moment that followed, she gestured toward her truck and continued, "But I should get underway now. I'm so grateful to you and Chip for making this transition easy for Toffee."

Ellen's face cleared as she gave a nod.

"Our pleasure. And I'm excited to break out my dancing shoes for the evening of the bachelor auction. That band you hired is one of Chip's favorites."

After a few more pleasantries exchanged, Lauryn was in her truck again and driving to her meeting with Gavin at the Broken Spur Ranch.

Heading south through the scenic beauty that came with this stretch of 287, Lauryn heard her former foster mom's words circling around in her head.

Not just *what* she'd said. But *how* she'd said it. Because Ellen Crawford wasn't a woman to mince words, or to share a story just for the sake of shooting the breeze.

Clearly, the incident she'd witnessed with Lauryn's father pulling over Gavin had bothered her enough to relate it. Almost as if she felt defensive of Gavin. Which stirred Lauryn's uncertain feelings about him all the more. During the years she'd lived in foster homes, she'd grown accustomed to reading the room quickly, trying to get a take on people in a way that even now made her prone to overanalyzing.

Maybe she was doing that now, picking at stray threads that didn't need unraveling.

The elevation increased before it decreased again, her truck feeling the incline more with the heavy horse trailer in tow. Still, she checked the time on her dashboard and saw she would arrive punctually enough.

No need to text Gavin in advance.

Even as she thought it, her truck's Bluetooth chimed with a notification from her phone, the connection informing her she had an incoming message from Gavin Kingsley. The system was even polite enough to ask her if she wanted the message read to her so her eyes could remain on the road.

Curiosity hummed through her, even as she felt a zing of kismet that he'd apparently been thinking of her at the same moment she'd been thinking of him. Foolish, really, given they had a meeting scheduled shortly. She should be relieved he'd remembered it this time.

Then the disembodied voice of her messaging app sounded over the truck's speakers, reading aloud to her.

"Hey, this is Gavin. Just checking in to make sure we're still on for this afternoon. I'll be in all day, so don't rush if your delivery runs long."

Lauryn's pulse thrummed faster, remembering the way Gavin had touched her the day before when they'd shaken hands on the deal they made. There'd been a moment—an infinitesimal shift of his thumb along the back of her hand—when heat had spiked all through her. A charged instant between them she hadn't been able to forget.

Now she would see him again so they could work together in close proximity on her event. Her stomach flipped.

Was that unease she was feeling? Anxiety?

It had all been her idea to ask him to be a part of the bachelor auction, so she only had herself to blame now, if the thought of being next to him for hours sent a sensual shiver through her. She could blame Gavin for other things, but roping him into this event had been all her idea because she'd known that the man would corral feminine interest for miles around.

Had she thought all her father's stories about him or all Duke Kingsley's disparaging remarks about his son would prevent her from feeling the influence of Gavin's charisma?

Just one touch yesterday had shattered any illusion of the kind.

Licking her dry lips, Lauryn reminded herself she had the very best of reasons for going forward with her plan: both to have Gavin in the bachelor auction and to maintain his help in organizing the event. He was a people person. A party person. While she was definitely not. His participation was crucial on so many levels.

No matter that they'd never been overly friendly toward one another in the past; he'd proven in their early meetings that he knew a lot about charity fundraisers and black-tie events since he'd been born into the Kingsley wealth. The fact that his father had disinherited him didn't suddenly void out the skills Gavin had honed over a lifetime.

He was good at this, and she needed him.

Clearing her throat, Lauryn spoke to the voice-messaging system through her Bluetooth microphone. "Send a message to Gavin Kingsley," she requested, waiting for the beep that indicated she could begin talking.

"The meeting is still on for this afternoon. I'm on my way now."

After the notification was read back to her, she confirmed the text and asked for the note to send, ignoring the sensation in her belly that felt sort of like butterflies.

It was only nerves, of course.

And since the therapy center she was dedicating in memory of her foster sister was riding on the outcome of Studs for Sale, Lauryn would do everything in her power to ignore the draw of the most notorious stud around.

Four

This isn't a date.

Gavin repeated the words to himself as he adjusted the place settings he'd arranged on the patio table built into his dock. He'd gone to some trouble to ensure the place for their meeting looked appealing, and he'd even ordered lunch in case Lauryn hadn't eaten. But as he reviewed the location of the table under a pergola, surrounded by container plants and shaded by ivy growing between the overhead wooden slats, he wondered if the sheriff's no-nonsense daughter might think it all a bit too much.

Especially since this meeting wasn't a date, damn it.

But he wanted to make her comfortable, and after he'd reviewed the meeting notes she sent him the night before, he knew they had a lot of ground to cover to work out the flow of the event. Then, afterward, he had a plan for drawing out the conversation. Maybe weave the talk around to the time she'd worked for his dad.

Something he wouldn't be able to do if she disappeared as soon as their business concluded.

He didn't have any longer to wonder about the setup, however, as a moment later, a dust cloud on the road leading to the driveway alerted him to Lauryn's arrival. Gavin jogged away from the dock to meet her, tempering his thoughts with reminders that he was only spending time with her to find out what she knew about his disinheritance.

And if she'd contributed to it in any way with her skewed view of him.

Yet as he rounded the corner of the detached garage to see Lauryn step out of her pickup truck in snug-fitting black jeans and work boots, a pink-and-gray flannel shirt tucked in on one side to reveal the narrow waist beneath it, Gavin struggled to recall those good intentions. Didn't matter that she was dressed for ranch work after the horse delivery, her face free of makeup and her chestnut waves bound into a ponytail. Or that she carried a binder that was surely full of tasks for them to accomplish. Gavin could only think she looked good enough to eat.

Preferably in slow, savoring mouthfuls.

"Hello, Gavin." Greeting him with a wave, she paused near the hitch for her horse trailer to rewrap a length of excess security chain that had come unhooked. "I'm surprised Rocco didn't come out to say hello too."

"If he was here, I'm positive he would have beaten

me to you." He gestured for her to walk with him toward the trout pond, and she kept pace beside him. "But the foreman lured him out to help drive the horses to the summer pasture. The broodmares are all even-tempered and easy to move, but Rocco likes to keep up his skills."

"This must be a busy time for the breeding program," she observed, her step stalling as her hazel eyes fixed on their destination. "Will we be working outside?"

"That was the plan." The spring had been mild, and he'd assumed that—like him—she probably worked out of doors often enough to be accustomed to the temperatures. "But we can relocate easily enough—"

"No need. This is perfect." A smile hitched at the corner of her lips as she recommenced moving toward the dock perched at the edge of his trout pond. "I just wasn't expecting anything so charming. What an ideal backyard."

"I spent a lot of time making sure this place was exactly the way I wanted it." He felt the tide of bitterness rising at the thought of leaving Silent Spring, the home and grounds personalized in every way. But since he didn't want to talk about that yet, he quickly switched topics. "So this morning's adoption went well? I know sometimes it can take a horse a while to settle down after a trailer ride."

He waved her ahead of him as they reached the cobblestone path that wound around a firepit and then up to the bi-level dock over the pond. The patio table under the pergola had been built closer to a storage shed where he kept fishing gear and lawn equipment, while the lower deck held two Adirondack chairs positioned side by side, looking out over the pond and the river beyond.

"Toffee couldn't be happier," she reported as she trailed one palm along the blooming clematis vine that wound up one of the pergola posts. Her touch released the soft fragrance of the pale pink flowers. "She managed the trip like a trooper, and she's in good hands in her new home."

When they arrived at the table, where he'd arranged place settings at two of the four chairs, he withdrew one of the seats on the bare side of the table for her.

"How's this? I thought we could dive into the meeting agenda and then, if we're not finished within the hour, we can at least take a working lunch."

For a moment, he studied her face as she took in the details—the linen napkins and simple white china on tan straw mats, the crystal water goblets but no wine glasses, the pewter jug of sunflowers in the middle of the cast-iron table. At least he'd had the forethought to leave his tablet and a notepad out, too, in an effort to show her he was serious about helping her with the event.

He knew he walked a tightrope with her, balancing his need to draw her out with her desire to nail down the details of the event.

When her gaze flipped back to his, her expression was guarded. Her tone even, if a little stiff.

"That's thoughtful of you. Thank you." Taking a seat in the chair he'd indicated, Lauryn set the manila folder she carried in front of her as she tucked closer to the table. "If we stay focused, I'm sure we can plow through this at a good clip so I'm not taking too much of your time."

Dropping into the seat beside her, he switched on the tablet, more than ready to finish up the work ahead of them, though for entirely different reasons. Lauryn might be plotting a quick departure from Broken Spur Ranch.

As for Gavin?

He already had a plan for luring her to stay.

This is just business.

Lauryn reminded herself as she reached for a raspberry on the small dessert charcuterie board one of Gavin's household staffers had brought them after a light lunch. The food had been delivered after they'd worked for about ninety minutes. She'd debated stealing away without accepting the lunch invitation, but that seemed unnecessarily rude when Gavin had offered so much of his time and expertise to help finalize the plans for the event day.

So she'd made quick work of a delectable chicken-salad sandwich from the tray of choices Gavin's house-keeper had offered half an hour ago, thinking she'd leave afterward. But by the time the small dessert board was delivered a few moments ago—laden with bite-size fruits, chocolates, macaroons and a salted-caramel dipping sauce—Lauryn worried she'd ventured into too-friendly terrain with a man she needed to be on her guard around.

Popping the raspberry in her mouth, she savored the burst of sweetness while she tried to gauge his next move. "This is so decadent. If this is how you conduct business meetings, I can only imagine how on point your dating game must be."

Gavin arched an eyebrow at her as he dragged a square of dark chocolate through the caramel sauce. "Spoken like a woman who is angling for hints about our upcoming date."

"Hardly." She bristled, face warm, as she snagged a macaroon. "Just observing that it's no surprise women line up to date you when you are such an attentive… er, host."

"Not you, though, Lauryn. You've been careful to avoid me for as long as I've known you." Leaning back in his chair, Gavin crossed his long legs at the ankles as he observed her. "I don't think you're won over by things like that."

"Maybe I go for substance over style," she teased, her skin prickling with awareness wherever his brown eyes lingered.

And while she would like to blame a cool spring breeze for the shiver that danced down her spine, she knew it had more to do with Gavin's heated regard. Somehow, digging into the macaroon didn't ease the renewed hunger she was feeling either.

"I think there's more to it than that," he argued, selecting a strawberry from the small pile on the board between them. "You've been opposed to me from your first day in Silent Spring."

A low-flying—noisy—crop duster overhead gave her an extra moment to consider his words.

"Now that's just not true," she said after a moment.

She hadn't known anything about Gavin for months
after the Hamiltons had taken her in.

"Isn't it?" An amused expression carved a dimple in
his cheek while a mischievous glint shone in his eyes.
"How else would you explain the way you sprinted out
of that 4-H meeting the first time you came to town?"

A humming sound started in the back of her brain at
the mention of 4-H. She'd had a bad experience there
the one and only time she'd gone.

Not that it was any fault of the organization.

She'd been visiting the Hamiltons before her adoption
had been finalized, and Mrs. Hamilton had been a local
group leader, so Lauryn had gone with her for the day.

"Lauryn?" Gavin straightened in his seat, his expression clouding. "What's wrong?"

He reached out to her, laying a hand on her arm.

The humming in her ears grew louder. She stared
down at the place where Gavin's fingers curved around
her wrist. It was the only place on her body that didn't
suddenly feel chilled.

"Nothing." Shaking her head, she didn't want to remember that time in her life. "I'm fine."

"You're white as a sheet. Should I call someone? A
physician or—"

"No." She laid her free hand over his where he touched
her. Gripped his fingers hard in hers. "It's really nothing."

And yet she knew the more she refused to acknowledge what was happening to her, the worse it would be.
She hadn't experienced a full-on panic attack in years,
but she recalled how terrifying they were. How it felt
like having a heart attack.

Even now, the noise in her ears had cranked up to full volume, drowning out whatever Gavin was saying to her. She watched his lips move. Understood he was worried for her.

Something about the concern in his eyes touched her. Anchored her, even.

So, keeping her gaze locked on his, she tried to remember the steps her old therapist had taught her. *Don't fight the attack. Ride it out. Try to remain in the situation.*

If she didn't give herself a chance to confront her fear, she'd never get over it.

Just thinking about the advice that had helped her in the past started to ease the vise on her chest.

"It's just a panic attack," she managed, becoming aware of the warm, strong palm between hers.

"How can I help?" He shifted even closer, squatting beside her chair so he could wrap his other arm around her shoulders.

The warmth of that touch permeated her flannel shirt, banishing more of the chill that had taken hold.

Comforted her.

"You are helping," she insisted between long, deep breaths. In her mind, she counted down the inhalations to make sure they lasted long enough. Then counted down the exhales too.

In another few moments, the sound in her head quieted. Her heart rate slowed down a bit. She became aware of Gavin's hand lightly rubbing her shoulder. It shouldn't feel so good.

But she didn't have the wherewithal to fight relief from the panic, no matter the source.

"Are you any steadier?" he asked a moment later, his brown gaze intent as he watched her. "Your color is a little better now."

"It's easing up now," she assured him, fighting the urge to lean into him more. To breathe in the strength and warmth of him. To take shelter in those strong arms. "Maybe I should have a drink of water."

If nothing else, it would distract her from how much she enjoyed his touch.

Gavin refilled her glass from a stainless steel pitcher on the table; then he passed her the tumbler.

"Here you go." He returned to his seat, though he'd pulled his chair so close to hers their knees still touched as he faced her. "I sure as hell hope I wasn't the cause of whatever brought that on."

How to tell him?

She remembered the advice about confronting her fears. It had worked well for her in the past, so she wasn't about to start hiding from the things that upset her now. Even if that meant sharing this part of her history with Gavin.

"You couldn't have known," she insisted, her thoughts returning to that long-ago incident she'd buried deep in her subconscious. The memory of it had only just surfaced, a forgotten relic of a time she'd tried so hard to forget. "I didn't remember that it was you with me in the tent that day."

Gavin's eyes widened. "Are you kidding me? All this time, I thought I'd offended you somehow—"

She shook her head vigorously, snatches of the episode returning one piece at a time as her mind's eye cleared. Vaguely, she was aware of the spring breeze on her face, lifting locks of her sweat-dampened hair from her temple. And Gavin seated across from her, his fingers still clutching hers while the small fountain in the middle of the trout pond continued to spray water in all directions, the soft swishing lulling her to remember a moment almost thirteen years in the past.

"That was my first panic attack," she said finally, forcing herself to meet his eyes. To speak the words that she once would have found impossible to confess. "I didn't know it at the time. I just felt this crushing weight on my chest and started running."

She couldn't even recall where she'd gone. But she did remember being back in a bed at the Hamiltons' house afterward, terrified they wouldn't adopt her after learning she was a girl prone to bouts of anxiety.

But they'd tucked her into bed with quiet words that it would be okay. That she was safe.

"I don't understand." Gavin cupped her chin with his free hand, tilting her face as if he could somehow read her if he could find the best angle. "If I didn't upset you, what went wrong? One minute, we were plotting the composition of a soil sample in order to determine forage yield in a cow pasture. And the next minute, you were tearing at the walls of that tent to find the exit."

Lauryn's pulse quickened again at the visceral memory of feeling trapped. Her airway clogged. Unable to escape.

But this time, she breathed through it, reminding herself she was safe. Free.

"We did a 4-H exercise that night," she recalled aloud, knowing she had to walk herself through the event that had triggered the first panic attack in years. And while she understood that Gavin was curious about what happened, her first priority had to be soothing herself. Only then could she explain any of it to him. "The junior and senior members worked together since the senior leader was absent."

"Right." He nodded slowly, confirming her memory of the incident, as his hand fell away from her cheek. "That year, we were still meeting at the main lodge of the old scouts' campground next to Twin Lakes."

"I remember cabins." She closed her eyes, seeing it all again. The small alpine lake in the Greenhorn Mountain Range. A fallen sign over the entrance to the camp. A handful of rustic cabins. A few tents pitched by the senior members as part of an exercise they'd completed earlier that week. "There was a big green tent that one of the boys said was the sturdiest one around."

Gavin laughed. "That would have been me. Bragging to impress the new girl."

Lauryn couldn't believe she'd forgotten the whole thing.

Her first time meeting kids she'd later gone to school with, and yet no one had brought it up to her for all these years? Then again, the 4-H group had been comprised mostly of students in the next school district over since both she and Gavin had lived on the fringes of their district. Maybe the club hadn't consisted of that many people who'd been in her life after her adoption.

"We ended up working in that tent," she recalled, a vision of sitting cross-legged under the center dome of the canvas roof returning to her mind. "Until a bunch of boys started shaking the posts."

An involuntary shudder ran through her at the memory. She'd been terrified from that point forward, her mind seized with panic that the canvas would collapse and she'd be trapped.

The way Jamie had been trapped the night Lauryn tried to save her sister. Another bolt of panic speared her insides.

Or was it grief this time?

Her hand went to her belly, clutching her abdomen. As if she could hold her feelings inside.

"Some of my friends decided to test the theory that it was the sturdiest tent around so they could show me up." Gavin's voice remained low and even, his hand still around hers. "They were determined to make me look bad in front of you."

Lauryn heard his words, the scenario making sense, even as she continued to see it unfold through her own terrified eyes.

"The roof looked ready to cave in on us," she said, her throat dry with remembered fear. "I don't recall anything after that. Not until much later, when I was back at the Hamiltons' house."

"You don't?" Gavin's dark eyebrows crinkled in confusion before his expression cleared again. "Do you want me to tell you what happened after that?"

"Yes, please." She forced herself to nod, even though she didn't really want to know. Sometimes it was easier not to dwell on the confusing and scary parts of the past.

"You looked straight at me." Gavin's steady voice anchored her as much as his touch. "And your face went as white as it did today. Your lips moved, but no sound came out. I moved toward you because I was worried, but then you spun out of my reach and tore out of the tent. For a moment, you battled with the flap near the door, catching your foot on it before scrambling away."

His forehead crumpled as he related the story, as if the remembered worry was still cause for concern.

"I figured you hated me," he continued when she didn't reply. "From that moment on. Later, when you moved into Silent Spring permanently, those same friends that were with us that day egged me into driving over to your place one night to see if you really did think I was the devil incarnate."

She swung on him then, putting the pieces together. "The night you rode four-wheelers through Dad's fields?"

He rolled his eyes. "Yeah. Well. That part was unintentional, but that was the level of smarts we had at fifteen."

Lauryn struggled to make sense of the events through Gavin's eyes, reseeing their history in a completely different light. Not that it mattered much. Gavin remained a ladies' man and a player, a guy used to having people fall at his feet no matter what he did. She was still a woman struggling to make people like her, to do the right thing. To be a good person and deserve her parents' love.

To make up for not saving her sister.

"Lauryn?" Gavin's voice interrupted her musings, his tone gentle and intimate somehow.

His hand still holding hers with a tenderness that undermined all her good intentions where he was concerned. Because now that the panic had subsided, she couldn't help but notice the way his calloused hands enveloped hers. Nor could she stop herself from imagining those work-roughened palms skimming over more of her body. Her hips. Her thighs.

"I should go." She rose to her feet, tugging her hand free of his before gathering her notebook and pen. Her breathing coming too fast again but for entirely different reasons. "Lunch was nice, and I appreciate your help—truly, I do—but I really need to get going."

"So soon?" Gavin stood too. "Are you sure you're okay to drive?"

When her knuckles brushed her water glass, he caught it in time before it spilled.

Get it together.

"I'm fine, really." She knew her behavior probably seemed as erratic to him as it had over a decade ago when she'd run from that tent. But today had been rough enough without reliving the worst of her nightmares to him. Without her libido waking up and seeing Gavin in a too-sexy light. "We'll talk soon. I'll tell you about it another time, okay?"

Backing up a step, she bumped into her chair before she righted herself and edged sideways.

"You don't owe me any explanations, Lauryn. But I don't think you should drive while you're upset—"

"I'm not upset," she assured him, running an impatient hand through her hair. Everything she'd thought she'd understood about Gavin Kingsley had been disrupted by today's revelation. She needed to figure out what it meant. To decide if it had any bearing on the kind of person he was or if his character remained fixed in the category where she'd always placed him. As for the attraction? She'd find a way to put the lid back on that somehow. "I just need some space to get my thoughts together. I'll text you."

"I'm at least walking you to your truck," he informed her crossly, his hand steadying her at the elbow as she missed a step going up the flagstone path away from the trout pond. "You can allow me to do the gentlemanly thing there, I hope."

"Of course," she murmured to herself even as the warmth of his touch aroused more feelings she didn't want to experience toward Gavin. "I don't mean to be rude. I'm just—" She didn't know what she was about to say. But when she arrived at the door of her pickup truck, she felt saved from trying to make any more sense. "Thank you for all the help today."

His brown eyes saw deeply into hers. Full of concern.

And something more. Something she couldn't quite define.

"Text me when you arrive home, or I will worry." His voice was stern. Uncompromising.

She might have bristled if she hadn't appreciated the interest he took in her well-being.

"I will." She opened the truck door before he had the chance to do it for her. "Bye, Gavin."

Moments later, she was heading for home, recounting every moment of the new memory about a time she'd thought was well buried in her subconscious.

She hadn't expected to deal with memories like that today. And when combined with the need to be on her guard around Gavin, all her defenses had just sort of… caved in on themselves.

Not unlike that long-ago accident that had claimed the person she loved most in the world.

Pressing harder on the accelerator, she knew she couldn't outrun her demons. But just this once, she could put some distance between her and the newest threat to her peace of mind. Because even though it had been an old memory that had upset her today, it had been Gavin Kingsley who had talked her through it.

Gavin who had stroked her arm and brought her back to firm, stable reality.

Gavin who had wanted to know she was okay.

Her chest felt tight when she thought about how easily he'd slid into the role of protector.

Next time, she wouldn't fall apart so readily. When they saw one another again, she would be armed with the knowledge that he wasn't concerned about her so much as he was trying to work a seductive angle. Right?

Taking a deep breath, she let out a long, slow exhale

as she felt the world right itself again. She probably wasn't the first woman in distress Gavin had comforted, and she wouldn't be the last. With the pieces of her perspective slotting back into place—her world making sense once more—Lauryn thrust all thoughts of Gavin to the back of her mind.

Five

Three days after his meeting gone wrong with Lauryn, Gavin backed his horse trailer toward the Kingsland Ranch's newest stables and braced himself for another potential failed mission—retrieving the highly ranked sorrel stallion he'd obtained for the Kingsland stud program.

A top-ten barrel horse sire for two years running, Streaking Saint was slated to be the cornerstone of the stallion battery. An athletic horse with impressive pedigree and an enviable disposition, Streaking promised to make Kingsland a small fortune.

Or he would have.

Except that Gavin had researched all the stallions himself, and he'd been the one to find Streaking at a good deal. He wasn't about to walk away from the horse he'd purchased just because his father had decided he wasn't worthy of the family legacy. He had spent too many years tying himself in knots trying to earn his father's approval. Then, he'd overcorrected that mistake, turning to bull riding and hell raising for a rebellious few years.

He couldn't allow his father to take up any more space in his head.

But considering how many ranch hands were on-site this afternoon, Gavin didn't hold much hope he would be able to load his stallion without someone alerting his brother. Quinton wouldn't care since he seemed genuinely angry about their father's shifty maneuverings with the will. Levi was another story, however.

As the oldest, Levi took his responsibility as family leader seriously. And he'd made it clear he wanted to keep the Kingsley family united under the Kingsland Ranch banner.

Something that stood a snowball's chance in hell of happening.

Satisfied with the trailer's proximity to the barn doors, Gavin threw on the brakes and switched off the ignition before stepping down from the truck. And while, yes, he'd readied himself for the possibility of running into trouble this evening, no potential confrontation with his siblings would be worse than how quickly things had deteriorated with Lauryn during their last meeting.

After sliding the big barn door open wider, Gavin unfastened the safety latch on his horse trailer and lowered the ramp, all the while thinking of the cryptic conversation that had gone in a far different direction than he'd imagined.

Had she really not recalled their first interaction at a 4-H club meeting so many years ago?

For years, he'd assumed that he personally had done something to upset her, something that turned her against him for good. Even though only a few years separated them in school, and Silent Spring was a small town, they'd never been friends. She'd always been distant toward him.

One of his theories had been that she was claustrophobic and blamed him for the tent almost caving in on them. Or she viewed him as a bully who somehow coerced his friends into freaking her out. Who knew? They'd been kids.

I didn't remember that it was you with me in the tent that day.

Her words had turned all his memories on their ear, upending the little he'd thought he'd known about Lauryn Hamilton. As for the plan he'd had to draw her out about his father…well, that hadn't gone as he'd hoped either. Next time he saw her, he'd have to work harder to drive the conversation and find the answers he needed.

Even though a part of him just wanted to get to know her better. Unravel the sexy mystery that was Lauryn. Because damn, but it had been difficult to pull his hands away from her once he'd started touching her. What started out as comfort had stirred a deeper awareness. He'd held her hand, and she'd peered at him with big hazel eyes full of gratitude, almost as if she saw something more in him.

Something meaningful that others didn't see. Especially not his father.

But that was probably just his imagination talking. Lauryn had looked at him like that strictly because he'd helped her through a panic attack and not for any other reason. He needed to remember that.

Now he cursed himself for spending his time daydreaming about touching Lauryn's soft skin and wrapping his arms around her. He had a job to do here, and the sooner he got what he came for, the better.

Walking into the trailer, he popped open the roof vents and straightened a heavy horse blanket on the bar that would help keep the stallion comfortable on the ride home. Then he retrieved a halter and lead rope before heading into the Kingsland barn.

The sweet scent of clean hay drifted toward him, the barn quiet since most of the animals remained outside in the pleasant spring weather. But deeper in the barn, in the last stall on the left, Gavin spotted Streaking Saint already stabled for the night. In an effort to help him transition to the new grasses in the Kingsland pasture, the staff had agreed to bring him into the barn at dinnertime and keep him there until morning to limit how much he grazed until he got more used to a different diet.

"Hey, buddy," Gavin greeted the horse softly, reaching to stroke the sorrel's neck. "How do you feel about taking a ride tonight, just you and me?"

At fifteen and a half hands, the stallion was sleek but well muscled, with the bearing of a show horse and the fire of a competitor. Even now, he tossed his head and whinnied as if to remind Gavin he was made for better things than standing in a stable all night.

Chuckling to himself at the animal's antics, Gavin opened the stable door to step inside so he had more room to slide on the halter. He slipped the nose band in place, then secured the strap behind the ears, making sure to leave enough room to keep the horse comfortable for the short trip.

He opened the stall door again and led Streaking out into the aisle just as a tall figure appeared at the entrance of the barn.

"Going somewhere?"

Levi glared at him, staring him down in his Stetson like an old-time gunslinger angling for a fight at the saloon.

A gusty sigh heaved from Gavin's lungs. He was so done arguing with his family.

"What does it look like?" He kept his tone light and tried to ensure his touch remained easy on the lead rope.

He didn't want to upset Streaking, who was still adjusting to a new barn and new routine.

"It looks like you're a damned horse thief, Gav, but I know even you wouldn't do something so rash." Levi strolled toward them, tipping the brim of his hat higher as he took in the sights around them.

The open horse trailer. The lead rope in the hands of the disgraced half brother.

"Leave it to you to take up the misguided-patriarch vacancy as soon as it came open," Gavin shot back, ticked off now and unable to hide it, even for the animal's sake. "But if you've conveniently forgotten who did all the legwork to find this horse and purchase him, then it's no wonder you consider yourself ill-used."

Beside him, Streaking danced sideways, tensing along with the man who held his lead.

"I remember who did the legwork," Levi insisted, his voice low as he came to a stop a few feet away. "Maybe you don't recall who paid fifty percent of the sale price?"

Close up, Gavin could see the dark circles under Levi's eyes. His jeans and work shirt were more rumpled than they'd normally be after a day on the ranch, his whole bearing weary.

Had Levi been losing sleep about the inheritance drama? For a moment, Gavin felt the tug of empathy. Of all his half siblings, he would have credited the oldest with the most scruples about fairness. Even as a kid, Levi had been the one to make sure Gavin got his fair share of Kingsley assets.

He'd sent Gavin back to his mother's house with extra toys those first two Christmases after Duke divorced his mom, asserting that Gavin deserved more presents since he didn't get to live with them full-time anymore.

The memory eased some of the starch in his spine.

"We went in halves on at least five other horses," he reminded his sibling. "But I'm only taking this one. That's more than fair."

Levi reached out to stroke Streaking's nose, soothing the horse's agitation. "And I'd appreciate that opportunity to hammer out the details of what's an equitable solution with you, brother, but we need to do that in the attorney's office. Why haven't you returned any of the lawyer's calls about setting up a meeting?"

The reminder of the messages and letters from the law office only served to rile him all over again.

"I'm not interested in padding a lawyer's pockets to work out something you and I can agree on with a handshake." It ticked him off to think Levi and Quinton didn't trust him. "If you don't think I'll follow through on an agreement—"

"It's not that simple." Backing away from the stallion, Levi lifted both arms in exasperation. "How are we going to come to an agreement if we don't make time to talk through all the angles—"

"What angles?" Gavin asked through gritted teeth. "The only thing that's changed is that I'm not a part of Kingsland anymore. Simple as that. So offer me a financial settlement for what I've invested in the family business, and let's all move on."

He'd suggested as much on that first awful day when he'd found out he wouldn't be receiving a share of his father's estate. Before he'd walked out of the room, he'd told Quinton and Levi that he would expect to be reimbursed for every cent he'd invested in the stud program.

"And what about the rest of the assets? We just divide things three ways between you, Quinton and me?" Folding his arms, Levi seemed to size him up.

"That's your business, not mine."

"Well I can't do that since there are four of us who are entitled to Kingsland, Gav. Not three. How can we come up with an equitable settlement of the estate when we don't even know where Clayton is living, let alone how to get him back here to work with us?"

Swearing beneath his breath, Gavin felt the guilt rise up, rattling him at the knees. How could he forget about his own brother, albeit one who'd been in his life for all of a couple of summers? And of course, since Gavin hadn't lived at the ranch full-time after his parents divorced, he hadn't been around Kingsland very often during those summers when Clayton Reynolds had visited.

Quinton had been quick to mention their sibling right after the reading of Duke Kingsley's will, but Gavin had been so upset for himself, he hadn't paid much attention to the ways Clayton had been shortchanged too. To Gavin's mind, at least Clayton had the good sense not to mix up his finances with his father's estate, proving himself far smarter than Gavin.

"You're right, of course." Gavin laid a hand on Streaking's neck, taking more comfort from the animal than he was giving. "I thought Quinton was going to hire a private investigator to locate him."

"He did. And he found a last-known address at a little town in the Aleutian Islands, but we're not sure about our next steps." Levi broke off his explanation to nod toward the sorrel stallion. "You want help getting him loaded?"

Surprised Levi wasn't going to argue anymore about the horse, Gavin nodded. "I'd appreciate that." He made a soft sound of encouragement to the animal before leading him out of the barn. Once the steady clip-clop of hooves moved toward the trailer, Gavin picked up their discussion. "Can't the PI let Clayton know we need to contact him? Settle the estate?"

"We could." Levi swung himself up into the side bay of the two-horse trailer ahead of Gavin and Streaking. Once there, he withdrew a box of raisins from the breast pocket of his canvas work coat, giving the box a shake to rattle the dried fruit inside. On cue, Streaking's ears pricked forward, his attention on the treat as he walked straight into the opposite bay. "But since Clayton made it clear five years ago that he doesn't want anything more to do with Dad, we didn't know if that was the best approach. If the investigator doesn't handle the meeting well, Clayton could go off-grid completely, and we'd never find him."

Levi shared the treat with Streaking while Gavin began securing breakaway ties to keep the stallion steady for transport.

"And we still don't know what happened between Clayton and…" He couldn't bring himself to call Duke Kingsley *Dad* these days. "…your father?"

Levi tucked the raisin package back in his pocket before emerging from the trailer to help Gavin close the ramp and back door.

"Only Clayton knows." Levi settled his Stetson more securely on his head while Gavin slid the bolt closed on the doors. "Quint is leaning toward going up there himself to talk to him."

"All the way to the Aleutian Islands?" He didn't hide his surprise at the idea of Quinton setting everything else aside at Kingsland Ranch to personally hunt down the half brother who'd turned his back on the rest of the family. "Seems like a long way to go only to find out the guy wants nothing to do with us."

"He's still family, and family is too important to just walk away from without a fight." Levi's tone was firm. And more than a little pointed. "Besides, Quint wants answers about Dad and his reasons for trying to cut us out of one another's lives. He thinks maybe Clayton can shed some light on that."

Maybe.

But maybe Lauryn could tell them more about their father's motives too. She was a whole lot closer by than the Aleutian Islands; and in spite of his old suspicions about her, Gavin couldn't deny that he was eager to see her again.

Their last visit had altered some of his previous perceptions of her, making him less sure that she'd had an axe to grind with him from the very beginning of her days in Silent Spring.

"We all want answers," Gavin agreed, ready to be underway now that he had Streaking in his possession. In the barn behind them, he could hear the ranch hands bringing in some of the other animals for the night, and Gavin didn't want to answer any questions about his plans. "But I doubt Clayton Reynolds will have the first clue as to why Duke disinherited *me*. I feel certain that I wasn't involved in whatever went down between the two of them."

He dug in his pocket for the keys to the truck while Levi walked with him toward the cab door.

"Maybe not. But in the meantime, will you call the attorney back? At least bring their office up to speed on what you've invested at Kingsland so we can be sure we work out something equitable if I can't convince you to stay on board?"

"I'll give the lawyer a call." Levering open the door, he was already thinking about the call he'd make first, however. He needed to talk to Lauryn again. To press her for the answers she'd been unwilling to provide last time about their first meeting. Because even though he had a whole other set of questions about her time working for his father, none of that mattered until he figured out what had turned her against him. If not that first encounter when she'd had a panic attack—and hadn't even remembered he'd been there—then what was it that had made her wary of him all these years? Something she'd shared with Duke Kingsley?

"Thanks, Gav. It means a lot—"

"But there's no way I'm staying on at Kingsland." After slamming his door, Gavin fired up the truck engine while he spoke through the open window to his brother. "Once the bachelor auction is over, I'm leaving Montana, and I won't be back."

Breathing in the spring scents of a meadow in the hills above her horse rescue, Lauryn relaxed into spending time with one of the new mares she'd acquired the week before.

"What do you think, Marigold?" she asked the four-year-old palomino she was leading into the meadow for some hand-grazing time. "Is this a good spot?"

Marigold was already dipping her nose into the

clover, her white tail swishing gently to keep a few deerflies at bay.

Easing her grip on the lead rope, Lauryn laid a hand on the animal's shoulder, remembering how much she'd enjoyed this exercise during her own years as a patient of equine therapy. They'd been encouraged to gravitate toward the individual animals that felt "right" to them; then they'd learned more about their horses by grooming them and paying attention to what brushes and touches the animals liked best. In later sessions, they were allowed to spend time getting to know their horses, often leading them into quiet pastures for hand-grazing moments like the one she was recreating with Marigold today.

She still found the activity therapeutic when her spirit was unsettled, the way it had been ever since her lunch with Gavin that had stirred a forgotten memory.

Now she'd promised to share more with him about why she'd had the panic attacks, but how much did she want to confide in a man she was wildly attracted to but wasn't certain she trusted? Yes, he'd been kind to her when the icy grip of heart-racing anxiety had taken hold. Had helped her through it in a way that touched her to recall.

But was that kindness to women just a reflex for him?

She couldn't lose sight of the fact that she'd wanted him to go on the auction block for the bachelor event precisely because he was a notorious charmer.

"How much should I tell him, Marigold?" she asked

the grazing palomino while she twined her fingers in the animal's white mane.

Birds chirped and squawked in the quiet following her question. The only answer Marigold made was the gentle tearing of grass as she ate.

Lauryn tipped her head to the animal's flank, feeling the sun-warmed coat on her temple as she soaked up the peace of the meadow and the moment. She hadn't known how much she needed this time until she felt some of the week's stress ease off her shoulders.

Besides the episode with Gavin, her father had messaged her twice in the last three days, asking her to remove Gavin from the bachelor docket at Studs for Sale. She'd been too annoyed to answer with the manners and respect the reply warranted, but she'd have to craft an answer soon.

Even as she thought it, her phone vibrated in her back pocket. Not the quick pulse of a message, but the longer rumble of an incoming call.

Tugging it free, she glanced at the caller ID.

Gavin Kingsley's name filled the screen and instantly, her breath caught. Her heart rate quickened.

After a stroke of her hand along the horse's back, she pushed the button to connect the call, knowing she needed to speak to him soon.

"Hello, Gavin." She kept Marigold's lead rope in her free hand, unsure if she could trust the mare if she ground-tied her.

The horse seemed docile enough, and had had some training somewhere along the way, but she'd been taken from an older woman with more animals than she could properly care for. Lauryn felt sure Marigold hadn't been overtly abused, but she'd certainly been underfed and ill tended.

A condition Lauryn recalled well from her three years in the group home where she'd met Jamie.

"Lauryn, I'm glad you picked up." His voice, deep and resonant, had an immediate effect on her. Warm and smooth against her ears.

She remembered how he spoke to her softly when she'd been troubled and in the grip of the past.

"Of course," she said as mildly as possible, unwilling to reveal the way she shivered just hearing him. She leaned into Marigold again, soaking up the comforting presence of the horse. Remembering that she was talking to Gavin so that she could save more horses. Expand her rescue into equine-therapy efforts that would help more people. "I'm glad you stayed in town for my bachelor auction, so we're even."

"I called about that, in fact." He kept his tone light too.

Maybe he'd picked up on her vibe. Her desperation to keep their relationship professional and casual.

"I'm listening."

"I have an idea for promoting Studs for Sale on social media to reach more people and elicit more write-in bids. Do you have time to meet tomorrow so we can go over the specifics?"

She would love more promotion.

And more write-in bids for higher donations was music to her ears.

So even if seeing him turned her insides into knots, she needed to say yes.

"Of course. Where should we meet this time?" She wasn't sure about inviting him to the rescue. Her mother and father lived only a few miles from her.

She didn't need the added pressure of having her father show up in the middle of a meeting with Gavin.

"Would you be able to meet at Kingsland Ranch?"

She almost dropped her phone in surprise. The suggestion shocked her, given how adamantly opposed he was to doing business with his family anymore.

But she knew the ranch well, having worked there for two years.

"That's not a problem. Whereabouts?" The ranch was huge, with multiple homes on the acreage, plus the office headquarters.

Her heartbeat kicked up pace.

"I'll meet you at the entrance. I have a spot in mind, but I don't think it's anywhere you would have seen while you worked there."

"You're full of surprises. But I'm game. Can we do later in the day? I've got a meeting with a potential builder for the new therapy center at noon." She wanted bids ready so she could make an informed decision about the structure she'd need on her property once she raised the necessary funds from the charity event. "Will three o'clock work?"

"Perfectly. I'll see you then." He was all business as they said goodbye.

Lauryn knew she couldn't have asked for a better follow-up call to their awkward last meeting. Gavin hadn't mentioned the incident, and he hadn't pretended they had any sort of new intimacy based on the shared personal moments.

That was excellent news.

Yet long after she disconnected the conversation, she couldn't help but feel she was walking into trouble with him tomorrow. Because the more time she spent with Gavin Kingsley, the more he defied her expectations. The more he showed her he was someone other than the man she'd thought she understood.

And even worse?

In spite of everything she knew—or thought she knew—about Gavin, she couldn't stop thinking about touching him again.

Six

Today, he would stick to the game plan.

Gavin needed the reminder tattooed across the insides of his eyelids, apparently, because the moment he spotted Lauryn's truck heading toward him for their appointed meeting, he was already envisioning how she would look today. What she would be wearing. How she would smell.

Thoughts that ran counter to the damn game plan, which was to draw her out about the time she'd spent working at Kingsland Ranch. He couldn't afford to get distracted by how she wore her hair or by imagining how those chestnut waves would feel sliding through his fingers. Or draped across his bare chest.

And yet he'd been battling thoughts like those—and far more explicit images—for days.

By the time she pulled off onto the grassy shoulder near the ranch sign and parked her red pickup truck next to his, Gavin had himself under control. Although his eyes still took in the fact that she wore her hair loose and wavy over her shoulders as she stepped out of her truck. And yes, he may have noticed that her black jeans and gray button-down with the Hooves and Hearts logo showed off her lean feminine form to delectable effect; yet Gavin didn't let himself dwell on any of that.

"Thank you for meeting me here." He'd only been waiting for her for a few minutes, but he'd taken a seat on the tailgate so he could greet her when she arrived. Now he dropped to his feet and gestured toward the cab of his truck. "Are you comfortable riding with me? Your vehicle won't be disturbed here, if you don't mind leaving it."

"Sounds good." She hit a button on her key fob as she strode closer. Her vehicle made an electronic chime, the running lights flashing once. "It's all locked up."

He walked to the passenger side of his truck a step ahead of her to pull open the door. As she murmured a thank-you and stepped up to slide her boot on the running board, Gavin got his first hint of her scent. Orange blossoms, maybe. And something spicier too. He caught himself before he leaned closer to take a deeper breath.

Lauryn's fragrance would have to remain a mystery because he was sticking to the game plan. Once he was sure she was settled inside the cab, he shut the door and rounded the vehicle. When he climbed into the driver's seat, she was already buckled in, her legs crossed so that one black ankle boot bounced a silent rhythm in the space between them.

Was she nervous?

The thought cooled his heated thoughts more effectively than any mental pep talk he could have given himself.

"You said you had an idea for promoting the auction on social media?" she prompted him, glancing his way expectantly as he steered the truck back onto the Kingsland Ranch entrance road.

He supposed he should be grateful she wanted to keep things businesslike right now when he was battling memories of how she'd felt the day he'd tucked her under his arm and comforted her. She'd been in his thoughts ever since, desire for her a persistent ache. Yet, when combined with the niggling sense that she was feeling anxious, he couldn't just take the conversational lead she offered. He needed to check in with her first, given the way their last meeting had ended. Lauryn had had a full-blown panic attack, and she'd left before he even understood why.

He didn't want to risk treading into uncomfortable terrain for her.

"I do. But first, tell me how you're doing. Is everything okay?" He glanced over at her before turning down a dirt road just past the hay barn.

Her eyes widened at the question, but her foot was still bouncing double time like her toes were conducting an invisible orchestra.

"I'm fine. Ready to work." Her tone was off, though. A little high and not quite steady. Perhaps she heard it, too, because she pasted on a wide smile before trying again, "Just really intrigued by your cryptic invitation today."

"I'm ready to work too," he assured her, giving a brief wave to the equipment manager repairing a tractor in the shade of an elm behind the barn. "But I wanted to make sure you're not anxious about anything."

As he spoke, he laid his palm on her ankle just above her boot. Her foot abruptly stilled.

His gaze flicked briefly toward her face.

"Oh, right." Her hazel eyes darted from his, her cheeks flushing a pale pink as the truck trundled over a pothole. "Possibly, I'm remembering the awkward way we parted last time. I hope what happened isn't going to…interfere with what we're trying to accomplish?"

Relief eased the tension in his shoulders. At least she hadn't been nervous to be around *him*. He could alleviate this particular disquiet.

"As far as I'm concerned, we don't need to discuss whatever spurred the anxiety attack again if it makes you uncomfortable." He told himself to move his hand away from her ankle, where it still rested. A dictate he would follow just as soon as he wrapped his fingers around her lower calf to give her a reassuring squeeze.

The soft gasp she quickly smothered sent a bolt of heat through him. His chest pounded with the need to follow up that sound. To explore what other ways he could make her gasp with pleasure. To feel that rapid breath rush from her lips to warm his skin…

"I appreciate that." Her words sent his hot thoughts scattering, reminding him he needed to stick to the plan.

Her voice cracked a little as she continued, "So. Um. Tell me about your idea to promote the event?"

This time, Gavin knew better than to ignore the conversational escape from the images flooding his brain. As they continued the short drive to the mountain overlook he wanted to show her, he tamped down his feelings to focus on work.

"I think we should do a big social media campaign," he began, ready to outline every last detail until his pulse stopped hammering in his ears. "We spotlight one bachelor every three days leading up to the event..."

As he spoke, he sensed Lauryn relaxing into her seat while she listened. No doubt she was just as eager as him to ignore the chemistry between them.

He just wished his game plan to ask her about her time working for his father didn't rely so heavily on personal conversation. Developing a rapport.

Because he could already tell the effort to learn more about her was going to mean battling this attraction that grew more potent every moment he spent with her.

Two hours later, Lauryn reviewed the notes on her phone. She'd opened a spreadsheet to compile a content-management calendar for the auction's social media properties, and with Gavin's help, she'd already scheduled the first bachelor to spotlight for the auction.

Now, seated on a wooden bench overlooking the western face of the Madison Range, she couldn't deny that he'd been a huge help today. When she'd first arrived, something in the way he looked at her made her wonder if his idea of a promotional opportunity had just been an excuse to see her. Her pulse had leapt at that look, and the attraction had simmered even hotter when she'd sat beside him in his truck on the way to the scenic look-out where they'd been working for the last two hours.

Then, when he'd touched her, she'd felt that brush of his hand everywhere...

Yet he'd only meant to reassure her. She'd been moved to learn he was concerned for her after her anxiety attack. The thoughtfulness had melted her defenses a bit, showing her that unexpected side of him.

Now, with her content calendar created—and with Gavin's hard work getting in touch with all the participating bachelors to schedule their features on the Studs for Sale website—she couldn't be more pleased with what they'd accomplished.

"This is brilliant," she announced, watching the Hooves and Hearts Instagram page explode with positive feedback after her post about the "Stud Spotlights" beginning the next day. Each of the bachelors had agreed to repost their spotlight material on their own social media properties, which would increase her reach exponentially. "I can't thank you enough for sharing the idea, and helping me organize it so quickly too."

Shutting down her phone, she sighed contentedly as she gazed out over the mountains under the cloudless spring sky. The view here was one of a kind, and Gavin was correct that she'd never visited this corner of Kingsland Ranch before. It had made for a perfect spot for working, even though they'd had to employ a Wi-Fi hot spot in order to stay connected to a network for scheduling posts online.

"My pleasure," Gavin returned, his head still bent over his phone, where he tapped in a few final notes on the page of questions he was sending to all the bachelors to answer. Each bachelor had been assigned a day on the auction website and was responsible for answering the questions in time to post them for a spotlight. "I sat on a charity board for a children's hospital last year, and they did something like this, featuring a few of the kids in their program. It really helped personalize the charity."

"You did?" Lauryn pulled her attention from the mountain range back to the man seated beside her, trying to envision him taking time away from ranching and his reputedly busy personal life to donate time to such a worthy cause. Then, as he lifted his head from his phone to arch an eyebrow at her, she felt embarrassed to have judged him so quickly. "That is, I didn't know you were involved in other charities. I know volunteering that way requires a lot of time, and I certainly appreciate all you've done for Hooves and Hearts."

Shaking his head, Gavin went back to tapping in a few final words on his phone's screen. "Contrary to popular belief, I don't spend all my waking hours chasing women and ticking off the local sheriff."

His jab was well-placed, so she could hardly be offended.

Though it did make her wonder how he'd come by his reputation.

"In that case, I hope the bachelor auction will help people get to know you better," she said finally, wondering how he would answer the ten questions they were sending to all the participants in Studs for Sale.

What more might she learn about this man with
hidden layers?

"Somehow I doubt it." Finishing his work on his phone,
he set the device on the far side of the bench. Then he
tugged off his Stetson and laid that aside too. He combed
his fingers through his light brown hair for a moment, letting the breeze play with the strands. "In my experience,
people seldom change their minds about their neighbors
once they've formed an opinion."

"That seems like a cynical view." Did he believe that
she'd underestimated him? Pigeonholed him into the
same slot as always?

"Does it?" He folded his arms across his chest while
he peered out over the green valley that lay between
them and the mountain range. Behind them, the rap-
rap-rap of a woodpecker knocked on the big aspen tree
that shaded the bench. "My father viewed my mom as
an interloper in his world, even five years into their
marriage. He never could see her as more than a domestic. An underling."

The bitterness in his voice caught her off guard.

She'd expected him to point out how frequently his
own character had been misjudged—by her; by her dad;
by his father, even. That he was more defensive of his
mother than himself spoke well of him in her eyes.

"I'm sure it must be painful losing your dad before
you were able to resolve those feelings." She remembered that Duke Kingsley had been a hardheaded man
with a mercurial temper.

"He certainly seemed resolved on his end." Gavin
shook his head as he dug one bootheel into the gravel

that had been laid around the bench. "He rejected my mom long ago. Rejecting me now… It shouldn't come as a surprise."

"I'm sorry." Her throat tightened for the emotions he must be feeling. The hurt that had to come with the shock of the disinheritance. Every instinct inside her urged her to cover his hand with hers. To offer her touch the way he'd given his to her during her panic attack.

But given how much she'd been thinking about touching him this week, she didn't want to risk acting out of desire.

She tucked her hands under her knees, keeping them to herself.

"He was judgmental. Too proud," Gavin conceded. "But there were still things about him I used to admire." The shared confidence made her feel closer to Gavin.

Again, she felt pulled toward him. Wanting to offer more.

Instead of giving in to the urge to touch, she shared a piece of her past that she'd rarely shown anyone else. "I was too young to remember much about my birth parents. They left me in a Billings-area homeless shelter to be taken in by the foster system. But I knew friends in my foster homes who experienced the loss of problematic relationships. I remember how they struggled with regrets over the things left unsaid."

In the quiet that followed her admission, she glanced over at him to find him studying her in that intent, see-right-through-her way that he had.

"I never knew that about you. That you'd been in foster care." Frowning, he sat up straighter on the bench. "When you came to Silent Spring, the sheriff told everyone they adopted a relative's child. I thought you were his niece, maybe—"

"No." She cut him off, unwilling to remember how adamant her adoptive father had been that she not reveal anything of her personal history with the friends she'd made in Silent Spring. "He felt it would be best for me to have a fresh start here. I know he meant well, hoping that if we all pretended my past didn't exist, I would somehow forget that it happened."

She'd kept her story to herself long enough, however. Perhaps that was why she sometimes felt called to visit Ellen and Chip Crawford in Twin Bridges. To be known for herself. To have her history acknowledged.

Yet even now, having revealed this much of herself to Gavin, she didn't plan to tell him about Jamie. The loss of her foster sister was a deep wound, and she could still appreciate the wisdom of not having that part of her story shared unless she chose to relate it.

"How has that been?" Gavin asked, calling her from her thoughts while the woodpecker behind them took up its rap-rap-rapping up the tree again. "Do you think the fresh start helped? Or did it feel like the sheriff was trying to mold you into someone you weren't?"

She heard an edge in his voice that made her wonder if he really wanted to know or if he was simply searching for more reasons to dislike her father.

"He's not a bad person." Rising to her feet, Lauryn moved away from the bench to take in more of the scenery around them now that they'd finished their work for the day.

Besides, the conversation was making her uncomfortable. Her parents had been good to her. A lifeline to her future, where she could help others who'd been through traumas with the horse rescue and equine therapy.

"I'm not suggesting he is," Gavin continued more softly, standing to close the distance between them. "I just can't help but identify with having a father who is only interested in an airbrushed version of his progeny."

The spring breeze stirred the branches of the aspen tree nearby, a few fuzzy catkins brushing against the shoulder of her gray Hooves and Hearts button-down. Overhead, the leaves fluttered in the wind, filling the silence between them.

All the while, tension coiled in her belly as Gavin drew nearer. His broad shoulders stretched the cotton of a well-worn blue T-shirt, the sight of his strong arms calling to mind how it had felt to have one slung around her the last time they were together.

"That's not fair, Gavin." Stepping closer to make her point, she laid a hand on his forearm. "Not to your father, and not to mine either."

"Isn't it?" He nodded toward a path branching off to one side of the clearing where they'd been seated. The grass was more trampled there, the dirt trail leading slightly down a hill. "Come this way." He took her lightly by the elbow, turning her toward the trail. "I haven't shown you the real reason I chose this for a meeting place yet."

Curious, she accompanied him, her skin still hyperaware where he'd touched her. The air grew cooler as they briefly entered deep shade to head down a set of woodland steps made from flat rocks toward another sunny clearing ahead.

"My dad just wanted what was best for me," she explained, hoping it was true. Sometimes she wondered why he wasn't as fully on board with the horse rescue as she'd once hoped he'd be.

Why hadn't her parents RSVP'd for the bachelor auction yet?

"What about my father? You worked for Duke Kingsley for two years. Do you really believe he thought well of me?" Reaching the last of the flat stone steps, Gavin pivoted to look back at her while she made her way down the rest of them.

His question was pointed.

And full of land mines she'd rather not pick her way through.

"That's not for me to say," she hedged, recalling her employer's tirades about his rodeo rebel son. "I was just an assistant, so we had a business relationship—"

Too late, she noticed how carefully he scrutinized her. How he gauged her expression.

"You don't have to cover for him, Lauryn. You wouldn't be the first person he made sure knew that I was a disappointment to him."

Her cheeks warmed uncomfortably, but she wasn't ready to deny his statement outright.

She hovered on the last of the stone stairs, not stepping down to the tall grass below because Gavin remained there, giving her no ground. Demanding an answer?

Frustration rose.

"Your relationship with him was obviously complicated—"

Gavin acknowledged as much with a scornful laugh.

She ignored it to continue speaking, her temper beginning to simmer. "—but you still have good relationships with your half brothers. And in my opinion, family is too important to just turn your back on them when times are hard."

What she wouldn't give to have her foster sister with her today. Did he have any idea how fortunate he was to have so many blood relations around him?

Although she didn't say that last part aloud, maybe he read the gravity in her eyes because he backed up, opening her path to stand beside him in another sunny clearing.

Her focus remained on him for long moments afterward. She saw the tension working in his jaw, the deep furrow of his brow as he weighed her words—or perhaps thought of his retort since he was hell-bent on leaving Silent Spring and Kingsland behind him.

Clearly, the idea of family didn't have the same hold over him that it did for her.

"My mother is my family too," he said finally, his expression easing as he exhaled a long breath. "And I guess it feels like, in slighting me, my father has slighted her all over again."

Understanding dawned. Or at least, more than she'd had before. As she thought about that—Gavin's fierce defense of his mom—he indicated the land ahead of them where they stood shoulder to shoulder.

"This is Mom's garden, by the way." He made a

sweeping gesture to encompass everything in front of
them, his other hand resting at the small of her back
to lead her nearer to the spot. "She loved to sit up here
for the view of the mountain range when she was still
married to my father. She planted the garden the year
before they divorced, and the perennials still continue
to flower year after year."

As he spoke, Lauryn tried not to think about the
intimacy of his hand at her waist, attempting instead
to focus on the explosion of spring colors some five
yards ahead. A cloud of blue and yellow butterflies
hovered over an assortment of blooms in pinks, blues,
reds and whites. The stone steps had led them into a
clearing with a completely unexpected rock garden in
the middle of nowhere.

Even at this distance, she could detect the tiny flowers
of white lilies of the valley around the perimeter. Blue
and violet strains of rock cress filled in gaps between
the rocks and other plants. Dark blue columbines grew
side by side with magenta anemones. Here and there, the
surprise yellows of a flower she thought might be called
baskets of gold broke up the pinks and blues.

"This is so beautiful," she said with soft reverence,
her every nerve ending alive from being close to him
while she savored the sensation of stumbling into an
enchanted place. "Someone must care for it still?"

Her pulse sped with awareness of him. His touch. His
warmth. Six-foot plus of potent masculinity.

Spying a dirt path lined with smooth stones, she
moved toward the entrance, knowing she needed to
break the contact with him so she could collect her

thoughts. Steady herself after the sparks of attraction had lit her up inside. Besides, she was eager to see the blooms up close.

"I do," he admitted, keeping pace with her as a hummingbird zipped past her ear. "Or at least, I did. I'm not sure what will become of it once I'm gone."

At the edge of the garden, one foot already on the path, she pivoted toward him. Confused. Surprised.

Only to find him standing very close to her. His chest was mere inches from her. She had to tilt her head to meet his gaze. Her senses were all on high alert.

"You'd really leave this behind after lavishing hours—years—of care to keep the garden thriving?"

He stared down at her for one long heartbeat. Then another.

Her mouth went dry at his silent regard. Her breath hitched as a hint of his scent—balsam and spice—teased her nose.

"It's still just a plot of earth," he answered at last, his jaw flexing again. "And one that no longer belongs to me."

Lauryn detected the pain in his voice.

Oh, he hid it beneath the bitterness in his tone. But she was beginning to understand him a little better. Starting to see hints of the man behind the charming mask he normally wore.

Resisting the impulse to lay her hand on his chest, she reminded herself to think before she acted. Instead, she turned to walk one of the twisting paths through the garden. Here and there, boulders served as sculptural accents. Shrub rosebushes hugged some of the stone paths. She could only imagine how beautiful the floral oasis would be by midsummer.

"Thank you for showing me." Running her fingers along a fractured gray rock that played host to hundreds of tiny purple rock cress blooms, Lauryn breathed in the mingled scents of the assorted flowers. "I can see why your mother loved this spot."

A hint of a smile tugged at the corners of his lips while a robin sang a cheerful tune from a nearby tree branch. Gavin idly pulled a weed from the flowers close to where her hand rested on the rock.

"After how things went the last time we got together, I thought it would be a good idea to meet in the most tranquil place I know."

Memories of their meeting at his house, when she'd spiraled into a panic attack and taken comfort from his presence, crowded her mind. Reminded her how his hand had felt on her.

Even now, his elbow brushed hers as he tossed the weed aside, the warmth of his arm lighting up all her nerve endings from just that accidental graze.

"Thank you for that." A breeze made a lock of her hair tickle her chin as Gavin's attention moved to her face.

His brown eyes dipped to her jaw for a moment before his fingers reached to slide the hair away from chin. When his thumb just barely skimmed her lower lip, Lauryn felt her heartbeat trip.

Restart faster.

She told herself yet again to back away.

To think carefully before she did something she might regret later. Something she couldn't take back.

Yet her toes were already flexing inside her boots, lifting her higher to meet his mouth as it descended toward hers. The moment spun out slowly. So slowly.

He gave her all the time in the world to change her mind while his focus narrowed to her lips. Yet with her heart drumming out of control, her skin tingling everywhere and her breath quickening, she couldn't have possibly walked away from just one taste of Gavin Kingsley.

So in the end, it was her who pulled him closer. Eyelids falling shut, telling herself it was just this once, Lauryn kissed him.

Seven

Lauryn's kiss was like nothing he'd ever tasted.

Soft. Sweet.

But underneath the tentative brush of her lips over his? A wealth of passion and sensuality just waiting to be explored.

Still, it was a wonder that Gavin could concentrate on kissing her at all when his head shouted at him that this was happening too soon. That Lauryn expected him to be a ladies' man and dole out charm and kisses like a major player. Hadn't he wanted her to get to know him better? To understand he wasn't the bad guy people thought?

He hoped this wasn't some kind of test to see how fast he could cave to his baser instincts.

Even as the thought crossed his mind—troubling as hell—she made a sexy little sound, half breathy gasp and half throaty moan, that shut down everything else in his head. Because in spite of everything, he recognized that sound for what it was.

A hot and needy demand.

One he would be damned if he could ignore.

Especially with her fingers scrabbling at his T-shirt, the curve of her breasts flattening against his chest. Gavin banded his arm around her back, drawing her against him.

Hard.

Just this once he needed to feel her, to know the shape and give of her body when fitted to his. He lifted her slightly, bending her back over his arm. He groaned when her hips met his, the sound mingling with Lauryn's hungry murmur of approval.

Wasn't it? Approval?

Remembering they were in the middle of his mother's garden and that he was supposed to be showing her his honorable side, all while figuring out what she knew about his father's plans to disinherit him, Gavin forced himself to break the kiss.

He wrenched his eyes open in time to see her lashes flutter more slowly, like a dreamer awakened.

Her damp lips were swollen and pink, her cheeks flushed as her gaze sought his. He employed every ounce of his restraint not to sink right back into that kiss.

"What is it? Why did you stop?" Confusion clouded her hazel gaze.

There had been a time in his life when seeing a woman look at him that way, combined with words that urged him on, Gavin would have indulged them both without a second thought. But Lauryn wasn't just any woman.

And after a lifetime of having his character under-estimated, Gavin wasn't the same man he used to be. Gritting his teeth with the effort, he lowered Lauryn's feet back to the ground and released her.

"Was that a test?" His tone was harsher than he'd intended.

But he'd already taxed his restraint enough for this afternoon. He didn't have any tact left for his words.

"Excuse me?" Her eyes flashed with a different kind of fire than what he'd seen there earlier.

"You know I'm hoping to show you another side of myself." He shoved a hand through his hair, trying to recall how he'd failed at the game plan once again. "Did you kiss me to see if my status as a reprobate still applies?"

Her mouth opened in a surprised O for a moment before she snapped her jaw shut again. Her eyes narrowed.

"I don't play games like that," she informed him stiffly. She folded her arms as she backed away a step.

Retreating. Regrouping, maybe.

Making him feel like an ass for thinking there'd been more to her motives. But if the kiss hadn't been a way to prove to him that he was as much a player as ever…

Did that mean she'd been acting on the chemistry he'd always known was there?

His heart thumped hard in his chest. Too bad he'd just alienated her big-time with his question.

"Lauryn—"

"If it's just the same to you, I'd appreciate a ride back

to my truck." She moved toward the rock steps built into the hillside that led up to the lookout bench. "Now."

Ah, damn.

He'd misread things with her. Probably doomed himself from ever tasting her lips again.

As he followed her back through the second clearing, picking up his phone and hat on the way, Gavin realized that the idea of never kissing her again bothered him even more than failing at his one mission today.

Finding out what she'd known about his father's plans to cut him out of his will.

Fortunately for him, he still had the promise of a date with her in his back pocket. It could be his last opportunity to learn why his dad wanted to erase him from the Kingsley legacy.

Worse? It might also be his last chance to smooth things over with a woman whose kiss he feared would remain on his mind longer than any full-blown intimate encounter he'd ever had.

Two days later, Lauryn pulled into the driveway at her parents' house for Sunday dinner and willed all thoughts of Gavin Kingsley to the back of her mind.

She would have banished them from her head completely, but after two days of trying, she knew that wasn't possible.

Yet.

Parking in front of the second garage bay, where her mother's little-used compact car normally rested, Lauryn shut off the engine and checked her reflection in the rearview mirror. As she smoothed away a trace of flour on her cheek from the biscuits she'd made to contribute to the meal, she reminded herself that Gavin Kingsley would be out of her life for good after the bachelor auction.

She hoped the memory of that kiss that had scorched her insides would leave with him. Because it mortified her to know a fusing of mouths that had turned her world upside down had meant so little to him that he thought she'd merely been testing his bad boy status.

Swearing under her breath, she scooped up her purse and her covered plate of biscuits, then opened the door. Already, her father was stepping out onto the porch to greet her.

She steeled herself for an evening with him. Because while she loved her dad, she couldn't understand his complete lack of support on the bachelor-auction fundraiser. Bad enough he hadn't submitted the reply card assuring her of his attendance. But for his only response to be messages asking her not to include Gavin? That hurt.

She felt a little nervous about it. And yes, a bit hurt too. Those feelings, combined with her concerns raised from Ellen Crawford's story about the sheriff's treatment of Gavin, plus the recent panic attack about events she hadn't recalled before Gavin's reminder of it, made this Sunday meal seem more emotionally loaded than usual.

She had questions about all of it.

"You're just in time." Sheriff Caleb Hamilton was a big, burly man who'd served as an elected official in Silent Spring since before Lauryn's arrival. Even without his uniform, he carried himself with authority, his stern glances enough to make the kids in town straighten up and the drivers on Main Street slow down. "Let me give you a hand."

He met her at the bottom of the porch steps of the small stone ranch house, taking the biscuits from her as he kissed her on the cheek.

"Thank you. And why am I 'just in time'?" She followed him into the house.

The scent of a roast chicken filtered in from the kitchen. Along with another, harsher scent of something burning. And the sounds of pans banging while her mother loudly berated her oven.

"A cooking mishap, I think." Her father raised a brow as he stopped short of entering the kitchen. "I was afraid to ask."

Laughing, Lauryn took the biscuit plate back from him before he could steal one before dinner.

"Because Mom is so intimidating," she teased. "Just make sure the table is set, and I'll handle the rest."

Her dad saluted her before leaving her to her own devices, his playful gesture so reminiscent of her girlhood days that she felt renewed hope for the conversation she'd been putting off with her parents. Namely, were they attending her fundraiser or not?

"Hey, Mom, how can I help?" Lauryn wound around a kitchen cart that served as a makeshift island.

Violet Hamilton glanced up from where she knelt in front of her open oven, her short dark hair frizzy from the heat. "Oh, thank goodness you're here."

Setting aside the biscuits, Lauryn leaned closer to

assess the damage in the form of bubbling black goo on the bottom of the oven.

"Apple-pie spillover?" she guessed, seeing a pie already cooling on the open windowsill. She grabbed a metal spatula to scrape away the worst of the damage from the oven floor. "I can clean up if you want to finish the chicken."

"That's a deal," her mother said, smiling gratefully as she rose from her spot on the floor.

Lauryn set to work, not minding the chore itself but regretting that her mom's frantic movements around the kitchen prevented any predinner questioning about her father's state of mind regarding the auction. Violet was the soft touch in the household—the good cop to the sheriff's sterner approach.

Because even though Lauryn wasn't a kid anymore to stress about her dad's input on her life, she was also mindful of all he'd done for her over the years. Choosing to adopt her when she'd been an admittedly troubled kid after losing her closest friend in such a traumatic way. Later, he'd stood by her when she'd had panic attacks, traveling ninety minutes each way every week to take her to equine therapy. Then, more recently, he'd helped her to purchase the land for her rescue, allowing her to pay him back at a ridiculously low interest rate.

So the idea of disappointing either of her parents weighed on her heart, and she couldn't imagine ever outgrowing that feeling.

A few minutes later, the three of them took their usual seats around a weathered old farm table that had been one of the original pieces of furniture to survive the fundraising efforts of long ago.

After Lauryn laid her napkin across her lap and made quick work of passing dishes around the table, she debated how to tactfully seek answers to the questions that had been building up in her mind all week.

Before she could begin—actually, before she even cut into her chicken—her father spoke first.

"Lauryn, your mother and I were troubled to hear you've been meeting with Gavin Kingsley recently," he began, still loading his plate with mashed potatoes.

Her gaze flicked across the table toward her mother, who kept her own eyes on her meal. A signal she didn't wish to be involved. And, Lauryn guessed from her long experience in wading through family dynamics, a sign that while Violet hadn't given Caleb her approval for roping her into the "we're troubled" comment, she also wouldn't gainsay him.

Meaning Lauryn was on her own.

She didn't bother asking where he came by his information. Silent Spring was a small town, and her dad made sure to pick up his morning coffee every day from Red Barn Roasters, the best spot to hear all the local gossip.

Taking a sip of water while she considered her response, she decided to parry with a counterattack.

"Gavin has been helping me organize the fundraising event for Hooves and Hearts," she answered, slicing into her chicken. "Which reminds me that I haven't received your RSVP yet. You *are* attending, I hope?"

Her mother shot a quick glance at her father.

Something about the look on her mom's face made Lauryn suspect Violet was as interested in the answer as she was. And just like that, her stress ratcheted up a notch. It hadn't been her imagination that her parents were deliberately not replying to their invitation.

"We were waiting to speak to you about it first." Her dad gave her the same flinty look he used at traffic stops, his blue eyes cool. "I'm hoping you'll change your mind about including Kingsley in your list of so-called 'eligible bachelors.' You won't be doing the young women in attendance any favors by letting them bid on that piece of work."

Defensiveness for Gavin surged as she recalled his words to her.

In my experience, people seldom change their minds about their neighbors once they've formed an opinion.

No wonder he'd taken such a cynical view when her father spoke about him that way. Still, she knew a reasoned argument was the only way forward with her dad, so she waited while she took another bite of her chicken, willing away her frustration.

"I have two of the Kingsley brothers signed on for the auction," she said finally, meeting his gaze from where he sat at the head of the table. "Which one are you objecting to?"

Her mother made a choked sound that might have started as a laugh before she turned it into a cough. It was tough to tell when her father dropped a frustrated fist on the table, making the silverware jump.

"The only one with a police record," he shot back. "Lauryn, you know Gavin Kingsley was a teenage delinquent and has done nothing with his life but drag race and make trouble since then."

The anger in her dad's voice surprised her. She'd known he had problems with Gavin dating back to that time Gavin had driven into their fields, but she hadn't realized the enmity ran so deep.

"Half this town drag races at the canyon, including plenty of your friends, Dad, and I've noticed you don't mind looking the other way when they race." She'd been to the event once when she was younger and a bunch of her friends were going. The races didn't happen often since they definitely skirted the law, but they were always well attended. "You can't hold it against Gavin that he wins. And I'm not sure it's fair to say he has a record when he trespassed here when he was just fifteen years old—"

"Are you seeing him?" Her father's voice cut right through her words.

Even her mother looked up from her plate at the question, a strain of worry in her eyes.

Lauryn felt her face warm. Which was ludicrous since she was a grown woman who'd worked hard to build a life she could be proud of. One she would have hoped they'd be proud of too.

She didn't want them to worry, but she also couldn't help feeling cornered.

"You are, aren't you?" her father pressed when she didn't answer immediately. "I thought you were smarter than that—"

She dropped her fork, letting it clatter back to the plate.

"Excuse me?" She felt cold inside at her father's thoughtless remark.

She'd worked hard to overcome a lot in her life.

The nightmares that had followed losing her foster sister. The panic attacks. But also the insecurity of being behind her peers in school for the first eighteen months she'd been in Silent Spring. Her wounds from the accident with Jamie had put her in the hospital for weeks.

Afterward, the emotional recovery and therapy had taken even more time away from academics. So for this man, of all people, to question her intelligence…

"I have to leave." Lauryn rose from the table, unwilling to sit through a meal seasoned with insults. "Mom, I'm sorry."

"Honey, I didn't mean that." Her father rose, too, but she was already hurrying out of the dining room to retrieve her purse. "Lauryn, wait. We're just worried about you. That young man's own father didn't trust him enough to leave him anything. That ought to tell you something."

She could hear his heavier footsteps behind her as the sound of his accusations grew louder. Closer.

Plucking her handbag off the counter, she swung around to confront the big, bluff man she loved but who was as stubborn as anyone she'd ever met. And, as his most recent words replayed in her head, an awful thought occurred to her.

"Did you have anything to do with his father's will?" she asked, anger making her speak this time without bothering to weigh her words. "Did you help poison Duke Kingsley against his own son?"

Her dad stopped in his tracks. "Duke didn't need my help to see that one was a bad apple. And I don't plan to support any fundraiser that makes some kind of hero out of Gavin Kingsley."

He said the name like he had a bad taste in his mouth.

And even though Lauryn had known her father could be bullheaded, she was still caught completely off guard that he could be so adamant about this. There had to be something she didn't know about her father's history with Gavin. Some piece she was missing. Because his reaction was over the top. Uncalled for.

Cruel, even, since it was beginning to sound like her father hated Gavin more than he loved her.

"So you won't attend Studs for Sale even if it's *my* fundraiser? For a cause close to my heart?" She searched her dad's blue eyes, looking for the love she'd seen earlier when she'd walked into the house.

How many other times had she felt this way? Like she had to earn love because it was never just a given for someone like her, a foster child with problems. With a past.

Behind her father, she could hear her mother's murmur, as if urging the sheriff to a softer stance. But to no effect.

Her dad's arms folded across his barrel chest in a gesture easily recognizable. He was drawing his line in the sand here. If she had Gavin in the bachelor auction, she wouldn't be seeing her father at the event she'd worked tirelessly to organize.

And given the way her dad had always been the stronger voice in their parents' marriage, she guessed that meant her mother wouldn't be putting in an appearance either.

In that moment, she knew her choice, and it was an easy one. Not because she believed so strongly in Gavin, although she certainly had begun to see him as a much different person than her father and even Duke Kingsley would have had her believe in the past.

No. She knew what she needed to do, because she wasn't going to knuckle under to emotional extortion anymore. If her father didn't love her enough to overlook his own prejudices for one evening, then she'd rather not have his support.

"Good night, Dad." Tucking the strap of her handbag onto her shoulder, she pivoted fast and walked out the door and into the early evening.

Once she arrived at her truck, she gave herself a moment to lean against the fender. Closing her eyes, she tried to catch her breath after the confrontation.

All the while, wanting nothing more than to run back into Gavin's arms, consequences be damned.

But since that definitely wasn't an option after the way their kiss had ended, Lauryn pulled her cell phone from her bag and did something she rarely indulged.

Opening a message box for a group chat, she prepared to type an SOS to her girlfriends. She'd maintained some friendships from high school. Not everyone had stayed in Silent Spring since graduation, but a couple of them had returned after college to build a life in the town where they'd grown up.

It's been a day here. Anyone up for a drink?

Within seconds, she saw the text bubble dots that indicated someone was responding. A moment later her phone chimed.

Is this a not-so-veiled request for girlfriend talk therapy?

Lauryn welcomed the laugh that came with her friend's reply.

Possibly. Care to discuss after a margarita?

Five minutes later, she had a plan to meet with two of her friends at a bar on the edge of town. Sliding into the driver's seat of her truck, she backed out of her parents' driveway and headed south, not allowing herself to think too long about the fact that she was heading to a bar owned by Levi Kingsley.

One that his brother, Gavin, had been known to frequent.

Eight

Tipping back a longneck bottle of his brother's latest craft beer, Gavin welcomed the citrusy tang of the IPA as he took in the lack of business at the Stockyard.

A couple of young ranch hands from Kingsland sat at the opposite end of the old-fashioned mahogany bar from him. Gavin had stationed himself close to the doors leading to the back office. A bartender kept himself busy cleaning already-spotless glasses since there wasn't much else to do. The place was empty except for a few bikers and two tables in the back where some people Gavin didn't recognize—out-of-towners, for sure—kept up a lively game of darts.

The jukebox played a country rock song that couldn't quite hide the desolate feel of a joint that was usually hopping at this hour, even on Sundays.

A moment later, the door from the back office opened and Levi stepped into view, rocking his usual threads: a low-key suit with no tie that still seemed way too formal for a Montana bar on the wrong side of the closest incorporated town line. Everyone else in the place wore jeans and boots.

A funny thing, too, considering Levi was the most important rancher in town. But then, Levi had always gravitated to the business side of things, managing their father's wealth and diversifying the Kingsley assets. Hence the Stockyard, which he'd bought three years earlier.

Levi didn't look quite as much like his usual power-executive self today, though. In spite of the suit and an heirloom Breitling watch that rarely left his wrist, the guy had circles around his eyes that suggested he hadn't slept well in a long time.

Gavin understood the feeling well. Sleep was an elusive beast in the wake of their father's death.

"I'm liking the IPA," Gavin offered by way of greeting, raising his bottle as Levi moved around the bar to take the seat beside him. "Good job on this one."

"Thanks, brother." Levi nodded at the bartender, who was already bringing over a glass of water for the owner. Levi's preferred beverage when he was working. "Wish there was an occasional patron around to drink it."

"Right. What gives?" Gavin picked at the label on his brew, tearing into the face of the logo for Gargoyle King. The image was dark and gothic and had never been what he'd expected from his older brother. "Why is the place so empty?"

"Bad press from Dad's will is spilling over into all corners of the business." Levi downed half the glass of water, then spun on the saddleback barstool to look out over the vacant tables.

Gavin set aside his drink, trying to make sense of his brother's words. "Not possible. Who would give a rat's ass about what Dad—*your* dad—did with his money?"

He recalled there'd been a couple of mentions of the family's fortunes in local news outlets after Duke passed, but the coverage had been limited because they'd avoided probate. Everything had already been in trust for Levi and Quinton.

"Plenty of people," his brother muttered darkly. "You forget what a huge following you had as a bull rider— how much support around the whole state. There's been a lot of backlash against Kingsland businesses among people who see you as the injured party in the inheritance drama."

Gavin shook his head. Disbelieving. "Injured by Duke Kingsley, maybe. Not by you."

The party in the back cheered a bull's-eye shot as Levi shrugged.

"Your fans have actively called for a boycott of Kingsland businesses. Like it or not, they're trying to rally around you the best way they know how." Levi glanced his way briefly before adding, "The female fans, in particular."

Gavin cursed under his breath. He'd put that part of his life behind him when he returned to Silent Spring full-time, agreeing to help his brothers launch the stud service at Kingsland Ranch. But there had been a time when he'd been a fan favorite on the rodeo circuit, his popularity helped by a *Men of Rodeo* calendar he'd done for charity. And, truth be told, his interviews about winning had struck a chord with some people.

He'd made no bones about needing to prove himself as the underdog in a powerful family. Something he wouldn't have done now, with the benefit of more maturity behind him. But back then, he'd still been stinging from his father's criticisms of rodeo, insisting Gavin should have been doing something "more productive" with his life.

Which, in Duke Kingsley's mind, meant making bucketfuls of money for the Kingsland coffers by working for the family business.

"I had no idea." Gavin ran a hand over his bristly jaw, hating that his former supporters had made trouble for his brothers. "I haven't been on social media much this week, but I can log on tonight and tell people that boycotting you sure as hell isn't helping me."

Maybe he hadn't noticed the storm brewing online because he'd been too busy this week helping Lauryn plan her bachelor auction. Too preoccupied with sending out the questionnaires to the other bachelors and sharing ideas for promoting Studs for Sale.

Ah, hell, who was he kidding?

For two days straight, he'd been consumed solely by thoughts of Lauryn and the kiss he couldn't get out of his head.

"I'd rather you just sit down with Quinton and me—and Clayton, when we find him—to legally accept your quarter of the estate. We could put out a press release and assure everyone we've addressed the injustices of Dad's will and divided things evenly among us."

Levi's head swiveled toward the bar's front entrance as it swung wide, the last shafts of daylight slanting through before a new arrival.

Gavin took the opportunity to return to his beer while he considered his reply. He wasn't going back into the Kingsland realm again. His father hadn't wanted him to have any of it, after all, and he refused to ignore that final judgment from the family patriarch.

His dad had accused him often enough of not respecting authority. He would damn well respect the old man's final wish, and then he wouldn't have to waste another minute of his life feeling like he'd stolen a legacy not intended for him.

But how to make Levi understand when his brother had never stepped a toe out of line and only wanted to right their father's wrongs?

Just as Gavin set down his beer again, his brother elbowed him. "Gav, look who's here."

Levi's low voice should have been a warning. But Gavin took an extra moment to hand his empty longneck bottle back to the bartender before ordering another.

So the sound of a woman's full, throaty laugh from inside the bar caught him unaware. That sudden burst of mirth tripped over his skin, nimble as a tongue, both sexy and familiar.

The hairs at the back of his neck straightened. Awareness warming his flesh even before he turned around.

Knowing who he'd see.

Still, the sight of Lauryn Hamilton at a table near the front windows with two of her friends sucked the air out of his lungs. The last glow of daylight was filtered by a gray shade on the long pane overlooking the parking lot, but the dulled rays still managed to pick out the burnished highlights in her chestnut hair as she smiled over something her girlfriend said.

Lauryn wore a blue-and-white-print dress, demure and pretty, but the vee cut of the front gave him a mouthwatering view of cleavage as she leaned forward at the table. The high-top gave him an excellent glimpse of her lower body as well. Neutral-colored spiky heels made her calf muscles flex where she crossed her legs, one she braced on the barstool while the other tapped in rhythm to the country rock song on the jukebox.

"Damn, but she looks great," his brother observed from beside him.

Gavin spun on him. Tension snapped his shoulders straight. "What did you just say?"

Levi's focus narrowed on the table with every bit as much intensity as Gavin's had a moment before. Then, as if he sensed Gavin's regard, Levi dragged his gaze from the women.

"Kendra Davies," Levi noted more blandly, turning back to the bar for his water glass. "Just surprised to see her in town again after she relocated to Denver."

Relief coursed through him.

His brother hadn't been talking about Lauryn.

Now Gavin did a double take, noticing the other two women at Lauryn's table. On her right sat petite, dark-haired Hope Alvarez, dressed in jeans and a pink

Henley with her new veterinary business logo printed on the pocket. She'd just set up shop in the next town over. She'd made a house call recently for one of Gavin's mares, and he'd noticed her ease and skill with the animal even though she'd only been in business on her own for a few months.

On Lauryn's left sat Kendra Davies, a statuesque blonde wearing a fitted navy suit and staring at the phone in her hand. Gavin remembered her from school, though she'd been closer to Levi's age than his. He didn't think he would have recognized her if Levi hadn't been practically gawking at her.

He was about to inquire about that. Or, more likely, hassle his brother about it. But then two things happened at the same time.

First, Lauryn's gaze snapped up from her friends and locked with his. Almost as if she'd felt his attention on her.

That instant of connection, even if it was only a long look across the room, set the heat inside him flaring again.

But simultaneously, one of the dudes from the dart game in the back of the bar made his way toward the table. His intentions were clear from the look on his mug, which was somehow both lascivious and too confident at the same time.

Gavin didn't even bother to excuse himself from his conversation. One moment, he was seated beside his brother. The next, he was charging across the bar, having no other plan other than to intercept the would-be hassler before he got anywhere near Lauryn.

* * *

Lauryn couldn't imagine what had prompted Gavin to stride toward her with a look on his face like he was going to throw her over his shoulder and carry her back to his man cave, but something about that expression made her body tingle head to toe.

Lingering at the most delicious places in between.

"Incoming," her friend Kendra muttered, setting aside her phone. "But no one leaves this table until we finish what we came here for. Agreed?"

On her other side, Lauryn sensed her friend Hope nodding emphatically. "Absolutely."

Forcing her attention away from Gavin, Lauryn wished her heart would quit knocking around so hard in her chest. "Um. Sure. Okay."

"Girl," Kendra warned in her most severe tone, raising one perfectly arched eyebrow to glare at her. "*You* called this meeting. Stick to the plan."

She nodded, knowing her public relations–expert friend had a valid point. Beside her, Hope's eyes darted to something behind Lauryn's shoulder, just before an oily, unfamiliar voice sounded from that direction.

"Hello, ladies." The greeting came from a cloud of cologne, heavy on the musk, at the same time a hairy elbow planted itself on the table between Hope and Lauryn. "What are we drinking tonight?"

A young man's face followed the elbow as the guy settled a narrow chin in one hand to leer at Lauryn. Her first thought was that this was why Gavin had charged across the bar toward her.

Her second was a moment of dismay to realize Gavin

only had that caveman expression on his face because he wanted to intercede and not because he planned to bring her back to his lair and have his way with her.

Which shouldn't be such a letdown.

"No touching," Kendra barked at the newcomer. "Respect our personal space, please."

"We're good, thanks," Lauryn assured the guy as she edged away from him.

Only to find herself leaning into Gavin, who'd rounded the table to slide an arm around her on her opposite side. The warmth and strength of him—from his hand gently squeezing to the weight of his limb draped along her shoulders—sent a shiver through her.

"Sir," Gavin addressed Hairy Arm respectfully, even if he flexed his muscles like a junkyard dog's hackles. "The bartender has your tab ready for you and your party. You can settle it up front."

Hairy Arm straightened, taking some of the cologne cloud—mercifully—with him. "We're not leaving—"

"You will be if you don't allow these ladies to enjoy their evening in peace," Gavin warned, his arm still wrapped possessively around her.

The touch was for a good cause, of course.

He was helping her send the interloper packing, and probably doing a faster job than they could have managed on their own. Even Kendra, with her big-city street sense and willingness to go toe-to-toe with anyone, couldn't have ousted him as quickly as Gavin. Because even now, Hairy Arm huffed his way back to his own table, muttering curses.

Sadly, no matter how many strides the sisterhood

made forward, some misogynist creeps only paid attention when a fellow Y-chromosome carrier did the talking.

A moment later, the bartender arrived with an icy bucket of six longnecks from the craft brewery owned by the Kingsley family. Lauryn recognized the Gargoyle King labels as cocktail napkins and frosted mugs were passed around.

"Courtesy of Mr. Kingsley," the barkeep announced as he straightened from the task and nodded to Levi just before the owner disappeared into the back office. "Let me know if you'd like anything else."

Distracted by the free drinks, and curious about the way Kendra's harrumphed how "some people were too proud to come over to the table to say hello," Lauryn missed the moment when Gavin gave her shoulder one final squeeze and vanished again.

A new party had entered the bar, too, so maybe Gavin had stepped outside when the door was open.

She hadn't even had a chance to say thank you.

Or tell him she needed to talk to him. Not that she would have shared the conversation she'd had with her dad this evening. At least, she didn't think she would have. Maybe she just wanted to apologize for being one of those people who'd made up their minds about someone before gathering all the facts...

"Which do you want?" Hope was waving a beer bottle under her nose, her pink Henley sleeves rolled up enough to show off the colorful ink of the animals scrolling around one forearm. "The lager or the IPA?"

"Lager," Lauryn decided, attempting to shake off thoughts of Gavin to focus on her girlfriends.

If anything, her hormones racing out of control tonight was more reason than ever to seek advice.

"So…" Kendra cast a speculative look her way. "You and Gavin Kingsley?"

"Definitely not." How many times had she told herself she shouldn't get attached to the town's bad boy billionaire? Even without his father's inheritance, he was a wealthy man in his own right. She'd read his bio for the bachelor auction. She knew about his personal investments in his brother's start-ups. And his own business—the stud program—already had a staggering net worth, assuming he untangled it from the Kingsley family to keep a portion of it.

Streaking Saint alone would make him a very rich man.

Hope exchanged a wry look with Kendra across the table while the jukebox switched to an old country romance ballad. Then Hope pointed her beer at Lauryn and said, "Yet he just draped himself all over you a minute ago, and you didn't even blink."

Sighing, Lauryn remembered this was why she came. She needed the help and advice of friends. Especially this week, when she was already feeling the annual melancholy that came with the impending anniversary of her foster sister's death in another two weeks.

After making sure Gavin was nowhere within hearing distance, Lauryn's gaze snagged on an older couple who'd moved onto the Stockyard's small dance floor to twirl a slow two-step, their eyes locked on one another as if they were all alone. A hollow pang filled her chest.

Then she bent her head closer to her friends and told them everything. The panic attack, the kiss, the unexpected side of Gavin she'd uncovered and—toughest of all—her fear that her father had carried an old, baseless grudge too far.

What she didn't understand was why.

When she finished her story, Kendra gave a low whistle. Hope chewed her lip.

"Well, what do you think?" she prompted them, reaching for a second beer. She would only have a few sips. But the tale had taken more out of her than she'd realized. "I should ignore the hot looks, shouldn't I? Run for cover? I keep reminding myself that he has female admirers chasing him from here to Kalamazoo."

Hope laughed as she scraped her dark curls into a ponytail and tugged a scrunchie off one wrist to tie it. "Maybe so, but that doesn't mean he's chasing them back. You can't really hold it against a man for being charming and attractive."

"Can't you?" Kendra asked, though her attention was fixed behind the bar, where Levi Kingsley was deep in conversation with an older woman in a fringed jean jacket and black Stetson. "The Kingsley men all seemed to inherit their father's sense of entitlement."

Lauryn frowned, thinking about Gavin's determination to leave town and not take a cent from his brothers for the legacy that should have been his. "I'm not sure I agree—"

Kendra whipped back around to face her, setting her

bottle on the table with a too-hard thud. "Sorry. You're right, and I'm off topic. What I don't understand is why you don't just go for it with Gavin? You want him, and from the hot, possessive looks he was giving you tonight, it's clear he wants you too." She shrugged, her expensive-looking navy blazer hugging her figure as she moved. "You already know there's a chance he's a player, so just go into things with eyes wide open. Enjoy some fun while it lasts."

Lauryn hadn't expected a green light. She'd thought maybe her friends would share what they knew about Gavin. Or help her scour his social media for clues about the real him. Or—actually, she'd had no idea what to expect.

Then again, she'd only just begun trying to knit together a serious friend group in the last year, as part of her ongoing path to healing from losing her closest friend ever. This kind of thing—drinks with the girls on a Sunday—was new to her.

As was advice on her romantic life since, so far, the guys she'd dated had been safe choices. Sheriff-approved.

"Hope?" Lauryn turned to her other friend. Hope Alvarez was as down-to-earth as they came. Before she'd gone away to veterinary school, she'd raised her own sheep and goats. Even now, she bred award-winning sheep in her spare time. "What do you think? Am I crazy to consider this? Especially with Dad giving me hassle for reasons known only to him?"

A smile curved one side of Hope's lips as she spun her empty beer bottle in circles on the table. "Gavin is great with horses, so he can't be all bad in my book. Sorry if that's a weird metric for applying to guys."

"No. I appreciate that insight, actually." Lauryn's equine-therapy days had taught her that horses were discriminating judges of character. "I just hate that my parents have turned my friendship with Gavin into a reason not to attend Studs for Sale."

She hadn't realized until she said the words aloud how wrong that felt. How much it hurt. Or how much she'd counted on the support of her family. She'd worked hard to be someone they could be proud of.

Hope covered her hand, her silver rings a cool weight on Lauryn's fingers. "Your dad can be a good man and still wrong about this. It's okay to trust your own instincts."

The advice settled around her, resonating.

"I guess you're right." She squeezed Hope's hand. Then reached for Kendra's and squeezed hers too. "Thanks, you guys."

Some of the tension that had been riding her ever since the argument with her father seeped out of her now. The fun of the night out, and the soft guitar strains of another romantic country ballad, soothed her insides.

Just in time too. Because a moment later, she spotted Gavin heading her way again, his brown eyes locked on her.

Stirring her senses.

"Incoming," Kendra whispered again, only this time it wasn't a warning so much as an invitation.

A possibility.

Releasing her friend's hands, Lauryn licked her lips.

Ready for whatever happened next. Because as long as she kept her eyes open and her heart on lockdown, she looked forward to everything tonight had in store for her.

Nine

As Gavin made his way toward Lauryn's table once more, he assured himself his intentions were good.

Honorable, even.

He'd given her time to catch up with her friends, refusing to descend on her the moment she set foot in the bar like the jerkoff who'd hit on her earlier. But something about the posture of her friends told him they'd finished the intense discussion they'd seemed to be having earlier. The veterinarian was now pointing out some of the ink on her arm to the suit-clad publicist across the table while Lauryn swayed her shoulders in time to a country love song, her gaze stuck on an older couple who'd hit the dance floor for every slow tune in the past hour.

As far as Gavin could tell, he wouldn't be interrupt-

ing. And he really did just want to apologize for the way
he'd reacted when they'd kissed.

Stopping just short of her chair, Gavin rested one
arm along the back of the stool while he extended his
other hand to her. "May I have this dance?"

Okay, so his good, honorable intentions were easier
to accomplish if they could speak privately. If it meant
having Lauryn in his arms at the same time because
they were in a bar and she'd been swaying to the music,
that was just a happy coincidence.

"I'd like that." Her breathy words were a soft huff
against his cheek where he leaned in to hear her.

She slipped her fingers in his palm as she slid off
the barstool, her pretty dress hugging her curves as she
moved. When her hazel eyes locked on his, he felt the
spark that always ignited when she was near. Only now,
it felt hotter.

Because she didn't break her gaze? Or was it because
of the sexy little grin she gave him before she sashayed
ahead of him toward the dance floor?

Whatever it was, he couldn't ignore the subtle twitch
of her hips as she moved, the hem of her dress caress-
ing her thighs as the fabric swished. His heart thumped
harder while he scavenged around his brain for those
good intentions.

She spun toward him once she reached the wooden
dance floor his brother had built near a small stage that
featured live acts on Fridays and Saturdays. Tonight, the
jukebox and the older couple were their only company
as Gavin embraced her, dropping any pretense of two-
stepping his way through this conversation.

Lauryn looped her arms around his neck in return, her body drawing closer to his like she wanted to be there. She felt soft beneath the thin material of the dress, her skin warm right through the silky fabric.

"Are you enjoying yourself this evening?" Gavin asked, knowing he wouldn't be able to focus on the apology he wanted to make if he kept letting his thoughts wander down the dangerous terrain of how Lauryn felt against him.

"Yes, it's good to spend time with friends. I haven't made enough space for that in my life." Her fingers played idly with the hair at the back of his neck, and he wondered if she realized the effect she was having on him. "Thank you for the help ousting our visitor earlier. We could have handled it—"

"Of course you could have. But you shouldn't have to put up with being hassled in the first place." Sensation streaked down his spine from the featherlight touches of her fingers. "Especially when—as you said—you're out to catch up with friends you don't see often enough."

"You're right." Her smile unfurled, the sign of her happiness making him feel like he'd won something more significant than any rodeo buckle. "I appreciate not having to waste our energy chasing off some presumptuous stranger. It gave us more of our evening to talk."

He was curious about what that conversation had involved. He'd noticed—in the handful of times his attention had found itself fixed to her throughout the evening—that she'd been doing most of the speaking. Was something troubling her?

The idea worried him as they shuffled slow steps

around the dance floor. The older guy winked at them as he and his partner twirled past.

Gavin's grip tightened on Lauryn's waist. He didn't want to be another presumptuous guy trying too hard to get close to her, so he didn't think it was right to ask her about her conversation with her friends. Instead, he reminded himself what he'd wanted to discuss with her in the first place.

"I owe you an apology." He couldn't stop his thumbs from grazing light circles where they rested just above her hips. "That's half the reason I asked you to dance."

"An apology? What for?" Her head tipped to one side as she gazed up at him, her full lips looking incredibly kissable.

The memory of her taste flooded his senses, the need for a repeat of that kiss urging him to pull her closer. Press all of her to him while he tested the soft give of her mouth once more.

"For ever suggesting you'd kiss me to prove some kind of point." He shook his head, still disgusted with himself about that. "If I'd been thinking straight, I would have known that's not something you would do—"

A ghost of her earlier smile returned. "Why weren't you thinking straight?"

The coy look in her eyes was a teasing aspect he hadn't ever seen on her before. He liked it.

Tremendously.

"Are you flirting with me, Lauryn? Right in the middle of my heartfelt apology?" Everything about the bar faded away, his senses narrowing to only her.

"Maybe. Is it working?" Her hazel eyes blinked up at him.

"Too well." He couldn't resist reaching up to trace a touch along her cheek. Tease his fingers along the line of her jaw. "Well enough, in fact, that I'm going to feel severely disappointed if it's the alcohol talking."

She laughed, her legs brushing against his. "Considering I only had one sip of a second beer, I seriously doubt that."

Desire for her surged. He had to remind himself where they were. That tonight wasn't his date night with her. He couldn't just act on the hunger she stirred simply by being in his arms.

What had changed between them to make her feel comfortable with him this way? Enough to kiss him? Flirt with him?

He knew she'd avoided him because of his reputation in the past. Had she really begun to see beyond the hearsay of a few people who had it in for him? Namely the sheriff and his own father? He'd wanted her to get to know him before the bachelor auction. Maybe she really had.

Gavin bent to speak into her ear through the veil of silky chestnut waves. "You can't begin to imagine how much I'd like to take you home with me tonight and show you how thoroughly you're affecting me."

The shiver that went through her trembled through him too.

When her eyes found his again, the green depths glowed brighter. Hotter.

"Maybe we should go out on that date I promised you," she suggested, her steps slowing to a stop.

He hadn't realized the music ended until that moment, his thoughts too crowded with images of her in his bed. Beneath him. Over him. Shouting his name on a hoarse cry as he teased her release free…

"A date." He repeated the words that sounded entirely too tame for what he wanted with her. He couldn't seem to let her go even though the jukebox switched to a fast-tempo country rock song. "That's a good idea. We'll talk through exactly what's happening between us. Figure it all out."

Her lips parted. Her breath came faster. She stood so close he could see the pulse pounding faster in her neck.

"Sounds like a plan." Giving him a jerky nod, she slipped by him to walk back to her table.

Gavin followed a step behind, wishing he had the right to kiss her goodnight.

But he couldn't lose sight of why he'd remained in Silent Spring in the first place. As much as being around Lauryn Hamilton tempted and tantalized him, he needed to figure out what role she'd played, if any, in him being disinherited.

And if she hadn't done anything to taint him in his father's eyes, Gavin still wondered if she'd known for years that he would be losing his place in the family legacy. Because that would hurt too. He'd spent so long trying to prove himself to people.

He didn't think Lauryn was playing games with him—he'd meant what he said when he'd apologized for assuming her kiss was a test. Yet something had shifted her opinion of him, and he wanted to know what that might be.

"I'll call you tomorrow," he assured her as he delivered her back to the table with her girlfriends, both of whom were now on their phones, heads bent together as they scrolled through their screens. He lowered his voice for Lauryn's ears only. "So you can make good on that promised date."

"Do that." She laid a hand on his chest, steadying herself to arch higher on her toes so she could speak close to his ear as well. "And you can make good on some of those things you mentioned to me too."

If there'd been any doubt in his mind about her intentions for this date, they were gone now. A fire blazed over his skin where she'd been touching him a moment ago, her words replaying in his head.

He'd wanted this damned date so she could get to know him better. To show her there was more to him than the heartbreaker reputation.

But right now, he couldn't imagine any scenario with Lauryn that didn't lead them into bed so they could excise the attraction still scorching him from the inside out.

Anticipation shivered over Lauryn's skin as she neared the small airfield where her outing with Gavin was set to begin.

Seated in the back of the big black SUV he'd sent to pick her up, Lauryn kept her eyes trained out the window, looking for her first sight of him. Or of the glider plane he'd promised to take her on today.

I think we're almost there, she texted to him now, remembering how nervous she'd been about the date at first when he'd changed the day two times. At first, he hadn't revealed why the days had switched, and she'd been nervous that he was having second thoughts about being with her. Then, when she'd pressed him about it, he'd admitted that he wanted to take her on a glider plane but that he needed the weather to cooperate for the best ride possible.

Once she'd understood the plan, the day swapping had all made sense. She'd agreed to meet him at the airfield since he had to transport his glider from the ranch, where he sometimes used it, to an airstrip. There he would meet a pilot friend of his to help him launch it so Lauryn and Gavin could land at a surprise destination.

Lauryn knew dinner was included at the other end. Since she'd never been on such an elaborately planned date before, she couldn't deny being excited. And that was before taking into account that she would be spending the rest of the day—and quite possibly the night—with Gavin Kingsley.

Besides, since the conversation with her girlfriends at the bar, she'd experienced a new need to embrace life. Not just with Gavin. But by taking chances. Seeing friends. Not trying so hard to please everyone—her parents especially—that she dimmed her own light. For years, the trauma of losing her foster sister had sent her down a path of caution. Safety. But maybe she owed Jamie better than that. Survivor's guilt never went away fully, but she could honor Jamie's life by living hers more robustly.

Her phone vibrated with an incoming message.

I see the SUV. Look out the passenger side window.

Scooting across the seat to the opposite side of the vehicle, Lauryn glimpsed the long body of a white fixed-wing plane, the nose painted bright red where it sat on a dark green field of grass. Two men stood talking beside the aircraft, one tall with broad shoulders who lifted his arm to wave. The other guy was shorter and wiry, with a pair of dark shades concealing his eyes.

A second, larger prop plane idled in front of the glider. The prop plane would act as their tow plane since the glider had no engine. Once the tow aircraft got them airborne, the prop plane would disconnect and fly back home while the glider simply…soared. She'd read up about it online and was excited to find out what gliding felt like.

Moments later, the SUV wove its way onto the small field, stopping near the prop plane to let her out. Gavin was at the door almost immediately, opening it wide to greet her.

"Are you ready to fly?" He held out a hand for her while a fresh spring breeze blew over her face, the sound of the plane engine rumbling softly.

"I'm ready." Slipping her hand into his, she realized how much she'd grown to trust him in a short space of time. From the way he'd comforted her after her anxiety attack to all the hours he'd volunteered for her fundraiser event to his defensiveness of her at the bar.

Minutes later, she was settled in the back seat of the

glider, staring up at Gavin as he finished his rundown of safety essentials. She knew where to find a parachute, though Gavin had assured her she wouldn't be needing one. And apparently she didn't need a headset either. He had a microphone and cockpit speaker, but those, too, he said shouldn't be necessary.

The pilot for the prop plane—Heath—was already seated in his aircraft, waiting for Gavin's signal that they were ready for takeoff.

"Here's your most important piece of equipment." Reaching into the back pocket of his jeans, Gavin shook out a brimmed white hat like a fisherman would wear. "Some extra sun protection."

Taking it, she noticed he also wore a brimmed hat, though his was a ballcap with the name of a small-town rodeo. The shadow it cast on his handsome face didn't begin to detract from how appealing he looked today as he double-checked her seat belt.

"Thank you." She fitted the hat to her head, tugging down her ponytail so the cap sat more comfortably in place. "Good thinking."

Her pulse throbbed faster, excitement building for the new experience.

"You're not nervous, are you?" Gavin asked, his brown eyes full of concern. "I want this to be fun for you, not anything to cause anxiety."

She shook her head, understanding why he wanted to be careful. She never had explained the panic attack she'd had at that first lunch meeting with him.

Reaching for his hand, she laid her palm on top of it. "On the contrary, I'm really looking forward to this. I recently decided I need to be a little more adventurous, so this comes at a perfect time."

A smile wreathed Gavin's face, and she could see how much he'd been looking forward to this day too. The spark of awareness was there in his eyes, reminding her she had so much to look forward to even after they landed.

"Excellent." He lifted her hand to his lips and kissed it before letting go again. "You're in good hands, Lauryn. I promise."

Her heartbeat was still jolting from the brush of his lips on her skin when he jumped into the pilot's seat and gave a thumbs-up to Heath in the prop plane.

At first, she only noticed the increase in volume of the plane's engine as it surged forward, the line between the prop plane and the glider stretching longer. Going taut.

A thrill shot through her once the glider lurched forward, bumping lightly along the grassy field as the prop plane rolled forward. Faster. Faster. Exciting. The flight…and the man.

"You're going to have the best view you've ever seen of Granite Peak," Gavin called back to her from his seat just ahead of her. All the while, their speed increased, the trees lining the airstrip seeming to blur before her eyes. "And it will quiet down for us to talk more easily once the prop plane lets us go."

She could hardly process what he was saying as the two planes lifted into the air, one behind the other.

Her squeal of delight split the air as they went airborne, the glider sliding slightly to the left of the prop plane as it pulled them high above the ground.

At first, she saw the tops of the trees just beneath them. But minutes later, they were well atop the pines, the view of the mountains and the Absaroka-Beartooth Wilderness enough to take her breath away.

"Wow, Gavin, you were right." She reached forward to lay her hand on his shoulder, feeling the warmth of him through his long-sleeved flannel and the cotton T-shirt layered beneath. The flex of his muscle under her palm sent a thrill of another kind through her. "This is incredible."

"Just wait until we separate and start soaring on our own. We're almost at two thousand feet now." Even now, he steered the rudder to guide them to the right of the tow plane. "Riding the wind currents is like nothing I've ever experienced before."

Considering Gavin had been a professional bull rider and a winning amateur drag racer, his endorsement of soaring as a unique sensation meant all the more. Giving her the sense that he was sharing something special with her. She was too caught up in watching him maneuver the glider, however, to comment on it now. She felt like she needed to store up all the sensations and take them all in.

"Here we go," Gavin warned her, reaching for the tow-release lever, something he'd pointed out to her in his overview of the craft. "We'll be separating now, and it will be just us and the wind currents."

Lauryn didn't feel anything different, but she knew the propylene line that had secured them to the tow plane no longer held them because the prop aircraft drifted down and to the left before circling back the way they'd come. The glider, in the meantime, continued in the same direction, the long wings tilting ever so slightly as Gavin tucked into a current.

The sky turned quiet as the other plane's engine moved out of hearing. Soon there was no sound other than her heartbeat and the air moving past them, no louder than a windy day.

Below them, she could see the imposing dark gray mountain peaks, some ridges still bearing snow. Between them, bright blue alpine lakes twinkled up at her like gems dotting the rugged terrain. And all the while, the glider tilted and swayed, silently cutting through currents she would have never known were there if Gavin hadn't explained how he would make the ride last. Apparently, he could stay aloft for hours when the weather was favorable for soaring.

"I can't believe how easily you move around the mountains," she called up to him, her voice slightly raised but no more than if she was sitting in the back seat of a car and talking to the driver.

"Keep in mind I've flown around this area many times. The ridges create really interesting airflow. But if I were going to take the glider to a new range, I'd research the currents carefully until I grew familiar with them." He steered the glider along a peak she didn't recognize, high enough that she didn't feel nervous about their proximity to the ground but near enough to the land that she could see some bighorn sheep scrambling along a rocky outcropping.

The view was spectacular. And soaring felt freeing.

She was shocked at the time when Gavin turned to ask her if she was ready to land. Checking her watch, she saw almost two hours had passed. The sun had slid lower on the horizon, although it wouldn't be dark for another hour at least.

"I'm ready." She knew she would treasure this experience.

He'd given her so much more than just a date.

"Good. Because I'm excited to share your next surprise." He tipped one glider wing lower, steering them to the right.

Stirring anticipation.

She knew dinner awaited them somewhere. And afterward?

Her mouth went dry at the thought of staying with him for the night. But after the glider ride, she was more certain than ever that the day wouldn't be complete until she'd lived it to the fullest—in Gavin's arms.

Ten

Gavin couldn't have scripted a better day.

He'd hated having to reschedule his date with Lauryn two times, but with the perfect wind currents today, he'd been able to land the glider precisely where he needed, a feat he could have only been certain of with optimal weather.

Now, hearing her happy laughter as he brought the aircraft down on a grassy meadow beside a mountain-lake retreat house, he knew he'd planned well. Satisfaction swelled in his chest as the plane skidded along the grass, as flawless a landing as he'd ever performed.

"I can't believe you!" she exclaimed from the seat behind him as he peeled off his cap and sunglasses before stepping out onto the grass. "You flew us so close to the surface of the water I thought I could reach down and touch a wave."

He hadn't been quite that close. But he recognized the exhilaration in her voice. Remembered feeling the same way plenty of times when he'd flown. And yet none of those past outings were as fulfilling as providing the experience for her.

"I take it you're a fan of flying?" he asked, extending his palm to help her out of the craft.

She still wore the fisherman's hat he'd given her, the wavy brim shading her hazel eyes as she looked up at him, the green depths glowing in the violet rays of the setting sun as it dipped behind a mountain peak. Her black jeans and fitted quilted jacket were the sorts of items he'd suggested for the plane ride since it tended to get cool above the mountains. When her hand slipped into his, he closed his palm around it and hoped he wouldn't be letting go of her for hours.

"I think I'm addicted. That was amazing." Stepping from the glider, she peeled off her hat and placed it beside his on the cockpit seat. "I can't thank you enough for sharing this with me."

With high pink color in her cheeks and her ponytail clasp slipping lower on her thick mane of hair, she looked deliciously tousled. He fought the urge to dishevel her further, not wanting to assume anything about the evening ahead of them when she'd only signed on for dinner. Besides, he'd planned one hell of a meal.

But it nearly killed him to see her full lips glistening where she flicked her tongue along them.

He swallowed hard, still gripping her hand as they stood in the grassy meadow.

"It was a pleasure." His voice sounded lower than normal, his thoughts straying to how much he wanted her. Clearing his throat, he forced his attention away from her mouth and turned them both toward the lake house he'd rented for their meal. "I've never flown with anyone else."

"I'd never guess that. You're so good at it." She peered up at the three-story stone-and-wood cabin perched on a narrow strip of land overlooking the private lake. "Why haven't you taken anyone else with you before?"

"I like the sensation of flying so much I guess I came to think of it as a way to unwind. It's always been a private thing for me." He paused at the base of the stairs leading to an outdoor deck. Glancing over at her, he squeezed her hand lightly. "But after our dance the other night, some instinct told me you might like the adventure."

"You were correct." Her pupils widened a fraction. She swayed closer. "It was exactly what I needed."

His heart thudded harder. Pulse ratcheting faster.

He couldn't fight the urge to touch more of her. Untwining his fingers from hers, he skimmed his palms along her hips. Drew her closer.

"Not true." He stared into her eyes, refusing to look away. "Exactly what we both need is waiting for us inside." He nodded fractionally to indicate the three-story mountain retreat.

"Point taken." She bobbed her head in agreement, her

breath turning thready and uneven. "Let's go explore that. Right now. No more delays, no more waiting."

Her meaning was clear.

Thank goodness.

He had so many plans for this woman he hardly knew where to begin. Logic told him the faster he got her indoors, the sooner he could make good on every last one of them. But the way she looked up at him now, her hazel eyes dipping to his mouth, practically *willing* him to kiss her, he couldn't move just yet.

Just one taste.

Because he owed her a kiss to make up for that last one when everything went wrong afterward.

Banding his arms around her, he lifted her against him, bringing their bodies flush, her lips aligning with his. The soft cry she made at the contact echoed everything he was feeling inside. And yet nothing was going to distract him from kissing her the way he'd been dreaming about.

This time, when he covered her lips, it was more than a kiss. It was a claim.

One he'd wanted to make for a very long time. Longer than he'd ever admit to himself. The lush give of her mouth welcomed him, her lips parting. Welcoming. And he took everything she offered. More. His tongue explored greedily, memorizing the silky textures, the mint-and-cinnamon taste, the quickening of her breathing when he stroked his free hand up her spine to cup the base of her head.

For long moments, he teased and played, mouths

mating. Then, wanting more, he drew back to nip her lower lip, dragging it slowly between his teeth. Sucking.

He couldn't get enough of this woman. When his kisses trailed lower along her jaw and beneath her ear, he savored her soft pleas of "more" and "hurry," her breath warm against his neck where her head lolled to one side.

Only then did he realize how her fingers worked the buttons on his flannel, her hands shoving at the placket as it opened.

"Too many layers," she muttered impatiently, her touch slipping beneath his T-shirt to the bare skin. "I want to feel all of you."

Forcing his lips away from her skin, he edged back to look at her. "I want that too." Then, lowering her to her feet, he guided her up the outdoor stairs with him toward the deck and entrance. "Come on."

"Where are we exactly? Is this one of your homes?" she asked as she kept pace beside him, hurrying up the steps with her hand hooked lightly around his upper arm.

When they reached the wide wraparound porch overlooking the small alpine lake, he keyed in the door code.

"No. I just rented it for the weekend. I figured it might be easier for us to spend time together without the speculation from all of Silent Spring." He knew her father kept tabs on him, and he suspected the sheriff was even more vigilant about keeping a watchful eye over his daughter.

"You're right about that." She sounded concerned, but when he turned to look at her over his shoulder, she seemed to shake off whatever her momentary worry had been. "And the view from this place is beautiful. It's like we're all alone in the world up here."

Still clasping his hand, she paused after he opened the front door of the house, her eyes roaming the clear blue water that lapped the rocky shore near the house foundation below. Beyond the lake, a dark gray mountain loomed, the side dotted with green pines in some places and snow fields in others even though the weather was almost sixty degrees where they stood.

"We *are* all alone," he assured her, grateful to leave Kingsland and the complicated family dynamics behind him, along with too many people who'd judged him unfairly. "For as long as you want to stay here."

Lauryn turned toward him again, her gaze colliding with his. "Lead the way."

When the door to the oversize mountain cabin closed behind them, Lauryn didn't waste a second.

With the adrenaline from the glider ride still buzzing in her veins, she threw herself into Gavin's arms before they even left the massive foyer. There would be time to explore later. She'd seen enough of the gorgeous view. The walls all around them now were dominated by huge windows overlooking that same perspective so that even indoors she felt like she was still perched above that clear blue lake carved by glaciers. Surrounded by the scents of pine and cedar.

Only now, she had Gavin's strong arms to anchor her, his hands roving everywhere, arousing every inch of her with his touch. The sensations he stirred felt so good, so dizzying and sweet, that her legs trembled beneath her.

"I haven't stopped thinking about you since that night at the bar," she confided, her hands picking up where they'd left off outside, gliding along his abs just beneath the hem of his T-shirt.

"I haven't quit thinking of you since that kiss in the garden." His voice was a low growl in her ear as he captured her wandering hands in his. "Which means I've had plenty of sleepless nights to consider just how I want to do this."

A shiver vibrated through her at the sensual promise inherent in those words. Or maybe it was from the way his fingers gently restrained her wrists.

"A man with a plan," she mused, unable to keep herself from canting closer, stepping between his thighs so their legs brushed. Her belly grazed the impressive length of his erection on the other side of his zipper, the contact making her blood sizzle. "Care to share?"

"Since I only have the promise of one date with you, one night, I can't rush. I won't hurry. Not when I need you to remember this for a long, long time afterward."

Her knees turned liquid as they faltered beneath her.

Not just from the rush of pure longing for whatever he had in store for her. But also from the jolt of a sudden fear that once would never be enough to satiate everything she wanted from him.

For a moment, she wondered if she should renegotiate terms. Suggest they not worry about a time limit for this. But she'd only made up her mind to enjoy the connection. Seeing him again this way in the future would make it more difficult to tell where the fun ended and a relationship began.

Something she wasn't ready for.

"But I want you," she told him simply. Honestly. "It's not rushing if we spend all night indulging each other. And we could start right here." Glancing around to get her bearings, she saw they were mere steps away from a sunken living area. Leather couches rested at angles to one another, positioned to take in the best views. "On the sofa."

"I want you too." He hooked a finger in the waistband of her jeans, tugging lightly. Making the denim move against her in a maddening caress when she craved his hands. His mouth. "But if we start tearing one another's clothes off on that couch, I'm going to forget all about my good intentions for you. And I refuse to lose focus."

She might have replied, but he chose that moment to slide his fingers along the front of the waistband to the snap of her jeans. Flicking it open, he lowered it slowly, his knuckles grazing her in ways that made her waver on her feet.

"Ooohh." She couldn't possibly articulate an answer when his brown eyes seared hers so that she couldn't look away. "Gavin."

His deliberate touches torched her thoughts along with her argument, until all she wanted was to put herself in his hands. See where this night would take them.

His forehead tipped to hers, the warmth of his skin stirring her, along with the flat of his palm where he laid it over the black lace of her underwear.

"Will you come with me to the bedroom?" He whispered the question lightly through her hair, just above one ear. "Let me undress you and take my time pleasuring you."

Another shiver tripped down her spine. She'd wanted this. To quit trying to please everyone else all the time and embrace life. Experience. Joy.

"Yes, please." Her words were a rasp of air along her dry throat. "But, Gavin, it can't all be about me. I want you to feel good too."

"Every single thing about this is going to make me feel good," he promised, his brown eyes serious as he took her hand and drew her toward the back of the luxury cabin.

Anticipation sending her heart slugging against her rib cage, she followed him along the gray-stone floor through the sleek chef's kitchen, the dark quartz countertops and light wood cabinets mimicking the colors outside the tall windows, where daylight was quickly fading. A bowl of clear blue stones decorated a natural-slab dining table.

Every moment's delay, every second making her way through the large vacation home, had her aching for more. Wishing they'd stopped at the sofa after all.

Then, beyond the kitchen lay a main floor suite, its open double doors beckoning them toward a king-size bed that dominated the room. A stone fireplace took up one wall, while two sets of French doors with lake views filled a whole other side of the room. Here, too, the view was stunning, the lake still visible in the violet dusk. But as soon as they crossed the threshold, Gavin pressed a button on a wall remote to shutter the doors, blinds in the glass blocking views in or out.

Sealing the two of them into their own private haven.

With the press of another button, flames lit the gas fireplace, the orange blaze flickering to life to cast a moody glow over the gray-and-white quilt.

Anticipation sparked along with it, especially as she watched Gavin shrug out of his flannel shirt. Then he reached for the hem of his tee and raked that up and off his body, revealing a male physique so mouthwatering she remembered why he'd been a *Men of Rodeo* calendar staple every year he was on the bull-riding circuit.

But when she reached to touch him, he captured her hands. Kissed the knuckles.

"Now you," he prompted her, guiding her hands back down to her sides. "I'm dying to see more of you, Lauryn."

Was he? The idea tantalized her as he lowered the zipper on her black quilted jacket, peeling it off and tossing it on a leather ottoman nearby. Then, returning his gaze to her, he slid his hands beneath the long-sleeved shirt she'd wore, bunching it higher. Higher. Lifting it over her head to join the jacket.

This time, his eyes never wavered from her body, still clad in a black lace bra that matched the underwear now visible through the open zipper of her jeans where he'd touched her earlier. She didn't own much lace, and she hadn't worn this set before. But the effort she'd made was well worth it as his focus narrowed to her breasts, his pupils so wide she could only see a hint of the brown iris ring before his head bent to kiss her through the lace bra cup.

Back arching, she fed herself to him shamelessly,

needing more. Aching everywhere. His arms banded around her, her hips meeting his and teasing forth another ache, hot and urgent.

She twisted against him, pleading without words. He only answered by switching to her other breast, kissing and licking at her through the lace of her bra until she shrugged and wriggled her shoulders free of the straps. She didn't want him looking too closely at the back of her shoulder anyway, where a network of old scars lingered. The dim room and her hair kept them hidden for now.

"You're so beautiful," he said against her skin as he unfastened the hooks at her back. "Everything about you makes me want you more."

When he'd freed her from the bra cups, the lace fell free, exposing taut pink nipples damp from his kisses.

"I like looking at you too," she reminded him, hooking her fingers in the waist of his jeans. "It's only fair."

The hot skin of his abs twitched under her touch, and she had to fight the urge to stroke him through his jeans. Now that she'd made the decision to embrace this time with him, she found it hard to go slow. Especially with her heart drumming triple time and Gavin's sensual attention making all her nerve endings prickle with awareness.

"You first," he reminded her as his hands slid into the gap in her open jeans. "Remember? That's going to be my mantra tonight. Lauryn goes first."

He cupped her hips in his broad palms, igniting more shivers as he worked her jeans down her legs. When they stalled at her boots, he bent to remove first one and then the other.

She balanced herself with one hand splayed on his broad, naked back, marveling at the fact that this was happening. She was going to be with Gavin Kingsley.

And he wanted her to go first.

By the time her jeans came off, leaving her in nothing but her panties, she trembled everywhere.

Straightening, Gavin's eyes were molten until he noticed the way she shook.

"Hey." His hand cupped her cheek as he pulled her against him. "Is everything okay?"

"More than okay." She nodded fast. "I'm just...so ready. I haven't done this in so long and—"

He kissed her again, quieting the words that were awkward for her. Only when she forgot what she'd been saying did he pause enough to speak against her lips. "I didn't know. Let me take care of you."

She wanted to tell him that he didn't need to worry about it. That orgasms weren't a big deal for her and it would only stress her out to put too much emphasis on having one since hers were about as common as unicorn sightings.

Especially when she was with a partner.

But then he was kissing her again. Lifting her against him to carry her toward the bed. She wrapped her arms around his neck. And with his body rubbing against hers as he walked...she lost herself in the way he made her feel.

Aching. Hungry.

Wet.

When he lowered her to the mattress, she kept her hold on him, liking the way his stubble—a few days' growth, at least, shadowed his jaw—raked lightly over her skin. She arched into him as he lay over her, wanting more contact.

Instead, his heavy thigh pinned hers, leaving himself room to touch her through her panties. Circling. Rubbing.

Stars lit up behind her eyelids, it felt so good. So exactly right. And when he slid aside the damp lace to touch her slick heat, she felt waves of pleasure like an electric shock.

This man wasn't guessing or fumbling. He knew exactly where she needed his touch.

Her face heated. Her whole body heated as Gavin crooned in her ear, telling her how beautiful she was. How sexy. How much he wanted her. How very much he enjoyed watching her.

And a moment later, her potential release twisted and coiled, tightening her to the breaking point. Her breath caught. Held. Then, unbelievably, the release just…unleashed.

Pleasure flooded through her hard and fast. Over and over.

Her body undulated against his hand as he wrung every last ounce of her orgasm from her body.

Breathless, panting, she wanted to tell him what a miracle that had been for her. But when she opened her eyes, she saw the desire in his. The need. Sweat popped along his brow. Tendons stood out at his neck as he reached for a condom from somewhere. His jeans, maybe.

He left the condom on the mattress beside her while he raked his jeans off. She swallowed hard to catch her breath, wanting with her whole being to make him feel as good as he'd made her feel.

"It's your turn," she reminded him, reaching down to wriggle out of her panties.

His teeth were already on the condom packet.

A moment later, he had it rolled into place.

When he nudged his way inside her—inch by inch, to let her adjust to him—she wanted to weep from the pleasure. Everything about being with him felt so good. So right.

She knew part of that was from the hormones and the orgasm. But, oh God, having him inside her was amazing.

Once he was seated fully, she tilted her hips. His gasp thrilled her. So she did it again. And again. Soon, they moved together in sync, driving each other higher.

Rolling over to take turns being in control. At some point, he felt the scars on her shoulder and went still. He looked questioningly at her, but she placed a finger over his lips, silently asking him to leave it for now.

She wanted this night to be about pleasure. Living to the fullest.

Only when her legs were aching pleasantly did he flip her to her back again, his lips sucking at her neck. Gently biting. Sensation tripped down her spine as he held there, his movements faster. More intent.

When she wrapped her legs around his waist, he

reached between her legs to touch her the way he had earlier, his fingers sure as he stroked her again. Coaxing her body once more into that trick that no other man had managed.

"Gavin." She wanted to tell him it couldn't happen again.

Except the first waves of it were already stealing her breath. Her body clamped around his. Tight. Tighter. And then he was shouting her name while she thrummed with her own release, his body following hers into that blissful oblivion.

His chest heaved against hers. Her pulse hammered in her ears, the aftermath making her skin tingle and buzz. For long moments, she just lay there beneath him. Overwhelmed by her senses and the magic that had just happened.

She didn't think that was overstating it either. No one had ever wrung so much pleasure from her body before. Herself included.

A dozen slugging heartbeats later, Gavin rolled away from her, kissing her on the temple before he stood to clean up. Which gave her a little time to watch him as he moved around the bedroom, his bare skin bronzed in the firelight.

Her mouth went dry just looking at him. Thinking about what had happened between them tonight. What did it mean? What came next?

Questions—worries—piled up in her brain, one after another. She had no exit strategy for this. No clue how to "be" when he returned to bed. She'd spent so much time this week imagining what it would be like to live a little, but she hadn't really plotted out what would come afterward.

Her heart beat harder as he returned to her, holding a glass of water in one hand for her.

She melted a little more inside, her defenses nowhere in sight. Tomorrow, she would worry about how to be. He knew it was temporary, after all, and he'd done this kind of thing before, hadn't he? She'd just follow his lead.

For tonight, she had hours and hours in front of her to make the most of her one night with Gavin.

Eleven

Gavin cracked open one eye at a sound in the kitchen. The electronic beep of a coffeepot, maybe. He could smell the scent of java in the air.

It took a moment to orient himself since the sun hadn't yet risen after his night with Lauryn at the mountain-house retreat. Dark hung heavy in the bedroom suite. He'd shut off the gas fireplace at some point, so he couldn't see much now. Still, the cold half of the bed told him that Lauryn was no longer beside him. Her scent still clung to the sheets.

Memories from their evening together bombarded him. After that first time making love on the bed, they'd devoured the offerings delivered by a local catering company. The champagne and caprese salads were easy enough to open and serve themselves, but they'd decided to steam the king crab legs. They'd worked side by side in the kitchen, him preparing the shellfish while she warmed up the side dishes. Then they'd spread a blanket on the living floor to eat a picnic in front of the fireplace.

Only to shower together and repeat all the fun of their first time together and more.

Which made him wonder where she'd found the energy to be up at this hour. They'd been awake half the night exploring all the ways they could give and take pleasure from each other.

Now, after peeling off the covers and tugging on his jeans, Gavin brushed his teeth before following the scent of coffee into the kitchen of the three-story cabin. He saw her by the light over the range, her pretty face illuminated in profile as she lifted a steaming cup of coffee to her lips.

Was she already second-guessing their time together? He feared that might happen, especially when they hadn't discussed anything before they'd launched into one another's arms. He understood Lauryn wasn't the kind of woman to enter into a physical relationship lightly. He'd heard she'd dated in college, but there hadn't been anyone in her life in Silent Spring—serious or otherwise—as far as he knew.

And the rumor mill in a small town was relentless, so if there'd been other men locally, he would have heard something.

He dragged a counter stool toward him to take a seat, alerting her to his presence. "You're awake early."

A thin smile curved her lips briefly. "Sorry if I woke you. I was having trouble sleeping."

"It seems too early for morning-after regrets," he observed lightly, trying to get a read on her. "At least, I hope it is."

She was shaking her head before he even finished speaking. "Nothing like that." Taking a step toward him, she halted again. "Do you want a cup of coffee?"

"No thanks, I'm good." He pulled out the stool beside him so she could take a seat on the gray leather chair. "Is anything wrong?"

Rounding the island, she padded closer on bare feet. Her brown waves were gathered in a loose knot, secured by a pencil. She wore the jeans and long-sleeved black shirt from the day before.

"I've been rehashing an argument I had with my dad last week before I saw you at the Stockyard." Sliding into the seat beside him, her arm brushed against his, calling to mind all the ways they'd touched the night before.

Even after acting out their feelings for one another over and over again, just that graze of her body still stirred arousal. Sharp. Fierce.

"You had a disagreement with the sheriff?"

She raised a brow, giving him the side-eye. "You say that like my father is an easy person to get along with."

"Sorry. I just meant that it seems as if the two of you have such a solid relationship. He's so protective of you. He obviously loves you a great deal."

Lauryn fitted her fingers around her mug, as if trying to absorb as much warmth from the steaming cup as possible. "Thank you. It's good for me to remember that being overprotective is his way of showing love."

"Then why the argument?" he prompted, genuinely curious about her.

He didn't know when he'd stopped trying to pry free information about his own father from her, but he acknowledged to himself that Lauryn didn't seem like she'd had any kind of vendetta against him. No reason to share negative stories about him to his father in the years they'd worked together. The woman he'd come to know wouldn't have done something like that.

"We disagreed about you, actually." Lifting her eyes to his face, she studied him for a moment before raising the cup to her lips again. Sipping. "He and my mother are refusing to attend Studs for Sale because I've asked you to be one of the bachelors."

Disappointment weighted his shoulders. And yeah, maybe even a little embarrassment, which was crazy. He was long past the age of needing a father's approval to see his daughter. Still, the sheriff's disapproval stung. "I can't say I'm surprised. Your father has never made a secret of his dislike for me since that day with the four-wheeler."

"But why?" Lauryn shrugged, the loose topknot on her head slipping sideways. "He has encountered teenage hijinks without holding a grudge before. Why go out of his way to give you a hard time for years?"

He had insights about that, but before he could answer, she continued.

"For that matter, my former foster mother told me that she saw Dad pull you over before when you weren't speeding or doing anything wrong." Her speech quickened, her brow furrowing as she related the story that had troubled her. "Ellen even phoned the station to let them know they got the wrong person because it was her who was speeding that day, and her car was close to yours. But she said no one seemed to care."

Gavin covered her knee with his hand, squeezing lightly. "It's okay. Your father and I have a long history, Lauryn. But there's more to it than you might realize."

"I don't understand." She frowned. "How so?"

In that moment, her goodness—her belief in people—put him to shame. She genuinely didn't know what he was about to tell her. And seeing that made him regret that he'd ever thought she could have swayed his father against him. Or knowingly withheld information about the disinheritance.

"Duke Kingsley paid your dad to hassle me in an effort to steer me straight. Or, depending what day Duke told the story, he might say that he was simply paying to have me watched and protected. My dad wanted to be the first to know if I was making trouble." He rubbed the ache that started in the back of his neck, the frustration and anger with his father residing there in a tense tangle. "Although sometimes I think he only requested that information to justify why he always made me feel like an outsider in my own family."

Lauryn remained quiet for a long moment. Coffee temporarily forgotten, she had swiveled her stool to face him fully. Her eyes were wide. Disbelieving?

"Are you suggesting…" One hand went to her temple.

Massaged. "I can't believe this. You're saying my father took bribes from your dad to give you a hard time?"

"No, that's not what I meant," he rushed to reassure her, not wanting to paint her father in a harsh light. Gavin knew how much she loved and respected her parents. "I don't think it was any different than your dad moonlighting a security job to make extra cash. Plenty of police officers do that."

"Not during the same hours that they're collecting a paycheck from the municipality where they work." Her fist clenched on the dark quartz counter. Squeezing. Pounding. "That would be completely unethical to use his uniform that way."

Had it been a mistake to tell her?

"I'm sorry, Lauryn. I thought you knew about their arrangement."

"How?" She slid off the counter stool to pace around the kitchen. "How would I have known that? I thought Dad gave you a hard time because he was bitter about his cornfield all these years."

His stupid, misguided effort to visit Lauryn that first time had resulted in him driving over newly planted fields with his friends.

"That's when it started." Gavin knew because his father had been practically giddy to tell him that he'd better watch his step going forward. "And I'm sure your dad was an easy sell for the job because he was righteously pissed about the cornfield. With good reason."

He wasn't sure how he'd become the defender of Caleb Hamilton all of a sudden, but he knew it wouldn't do him any good to be the one to come between Lauryn and her father.

Blinking rapidly, she looked from him to the floor-to-ceiling window where the very first rays of dawn brought a rosy glow to the sky and the water reflected it.

Then back to him again. This time, her face was a mask. But her eyes were clear. Determination glinting in their depths.

And a distance that signaled their night of intimacy was over.

"I think I'd like to go home now." She brushed a touch along his upper arm. "I know we need to talk about what happened last night, but right now I'm too upset to think straight. I really need to talk to my father."

His gut clenched. That wouldn't go over well with the sheriff. Especially when he learned the source of Lauryn's information. Maybe it would be better to stick with her a while longer.

"I'll drive you." He'd left a truck here in preparation for their trip. And he'd need it later to disassemble the glider enough to transport it back to the airfield. "But if it's any consolation, now that Duke has passed, your father won't have any reason to keep tabs on me anymore."

The sheriff's payday had stopped when Duke died.

"Except he's still refusing to attend my event because you'll be there, so maybe there's more to his enmity than you know." Anger simmered in her words. Picking up her coffee mug, she walked it over to the sink and dumped the contents down the drain before switching off the machine. "Either way, I need to talk to him."

Gavin understood she wanted to leave sooner rather than later. But he regretted that they hadn't had a chance to sort out where things stood between them. With the bachelor auction around the corner, he would be leaving Silent Spring soon. Tomorrow, he had an appointment with a Realtor in Wyoming to look at potential ranches so he could start over without the long shadow of the Kingsland legacy hanging over him.

Part of him longed to remind her of that; once he was gone, she needn't worry about what her dad thought of him.

But another part of Gavin already knew it would be tougher walking away from this town after last night. Whether Lauryn wanted to face it or not, things had changed between them.

And he understood that the kind of chemistry they shared wasn't the sort of thing either of them would be able to forget.

Seated on the back deck of her parents' house with a cold drink and her laptop that evening, Lauryn waited for her father to get home from work.

She'd seen her mother just long enough to exchange hugs, but her mom had plans with her book club friends and had rushed out the door. Now, trying to use her time wisely while she waited to confront her dad, Lauryn double-checked the scheduled content on the Hooves and Hearts social media properties to make sure the bachelor spotlights were ready for the next couple of days.

She also needed to fill the hours of her days now as the anniversary of Jamie's death approached. For years, she'd had to pretend the date was just like any other so as not to upset her parents, who'd asked her to make a fresh start. Since moving out on her own, she'd tried to remember her foster sister in meaningful ways, but the day was never an easy one.

Scrolling through the posts now while a few hopeful robins hopped around the back lawn, she realized today had been Gavin's profile day. The number of comments on his photo and Q and A were higher than for any of the other bachelors.

Some sixth sense told her not to linger overlong on the comments. Reaching to take a sip of her water from one of her mother's World's Fair drinking glasses, she reminded herself that she'd invited Gavin to take part in the auction because he was popular. A charmer. He had a huge fan following from his rodeo days, and even an underground drag racing following from his appearances at races around the state. Yet the wealth of fire emojis—with lips, kisses and hearts coming in tied for second place—she couldn't quite look away from the reader reactions to the profile.

Gavin, I love you! I would bid everything I own for a night with you!

That was a common theme.

There were other, more graphic comments that, as the owner of the page, she needed to delete. Which was frustrating when she didn't want to wade through all the responses. Deleting quickly, she tried to speedread her way through the rest, just to make sure everything else was page-appropriate.

Her eye snagged on a commenter's name.

Camille7, with a white flower beside the moniker. Her senses tingled a moment before recalling that Gavin had dated Camille Jorgensen, the wealthy daughter of a British polo player who'd retired to a sport ranch nearby. Camille also happened to be an up-and-coming attorney, so she'd had dealings with the Sheriff's Department. Hence, her father.

Camille's comment read, *Gavin, I have good news for you! Can't wait to share when I see you at the auction. Get ready for a date you won't forget when I win.*

Lauryn's skin crawled, and she had to glance up from the laptop to remind herself she was just sitting outside on her parents' back deck. The robins were singing and hopping around playfully. An aspen tree fluttered in the breeze.

Anyone else would be thrilled to see Gavin had raised so much interest and potential money for Hooves and Hearts. That's what Lauryn had wanted. Wasn't it?

A sound from the house behind her startled her from her thoughts. A moment later, a shadow appeared at the door before her father opened the screen and stepped outside, his expression one of pleased surprise. He still wore his uniform—khaki from head to foot, a gold star on his chest. His head was bare, however. He must have dropped his hat in the kitchen on his way outside.

"Lauryn, it's good to see you." He clapped a hand on her shoulder where she sat, squeezing lightly over the place where her scars intersected. "I felt badly how we left things last time."

Her stomach sank. It ran counter to all her natural instincts to argue with her father. The man who'd given her a permanent, safe and loving home. Yet she couldn't forget what she'd learned about him. And she had to know if it was true.

"Dad, I have something I need to ask you," she began, closing her laptop and setting it aside.

"I hope it's not about the auction, sweetheart," he said as he took the Adirondack chair next to hers, the wood creaking with his weight. "I can make a donation, if you like—"

"Did Duke Kingsley hire you to keep tabs on Gavin?" she blurted, her nerves strung too tight to wait another minute.

The look on her dad's face answered for him: A slackness in the jaw that was normally a chiseled square. A shift in the blue eyes that usually looked right through a person. Then there was the long pause.

Her hand went to her lips, covering her mouth and the gasp of surprise. Not until that moment did she realize how much she was counting on him to deny it.

"Now, listen—" he began, but she shook her head, unwilling to hear a rationalization.

"Is that even ethical?" she asked. "Ellen Crawford saw you pull him over once when he hadn't been doing anything."

The chiseled jaw went granite solid again. "I suppose you heard this from the man himself?"

"Why do you dislike him so much? I've never understood—"

"I'll tell you why." Her dad sat forward in the chair so he could turn more fully toward her. "Because he plays fast and loose with people's feelings, Lauryn. Breaking one heart after another. I've seen him do it, just the way his mother did before him."

She felt her eyes go wide. "His mother?"

"Isla Mitchell was the same way before she married Kingsley. Playing with hearts and not caring—" He stopped himself, his face coloring in a way she'd never seen before.

Understanding dawned.

"You dated Gavin's mother?" She wondered if Gavin knew. Clearly, he'd known about her father's deal with his dad and had been aware of it for some time. How much more did he know about her family than she did?

"Yes, and she thought nothing of moving on when a better opportunity came along. Like mother, like son." The bitterness in her dad's voice was unmistakable.

Her heart felt a pang of sadness for her mom that her dad would still harbor such strong feelings about another woman.

"So you've paid him back by hassling him since he was a teenager." Gathering up her laptop, she rose from her seat, not sure she could hear anymore today. "I came here to learn the truth, Dad, but I think I've had more than I can take today."

Especially when her father's image of Gavin as a player fell so closely on the heels of all those social media posts she'd just read—including Camille's assurance she would win him and share good news on their date. Not to mention, she was shaken to think her parents' marriage might not be as solid as she'd once believed. Had her mother been a rebound relationship rather than true love?

Her stomach knotted as her dad rose to argue with her, but perhaps he recognized the expression on her face as that of a woman who had all she could take today, because he huffed a heavy sigh and nodded.

"Gavin Kingsley will be leaving town soon enough anyhow." Her dad folded his arms over his barrel chest as he watched her walk down the steps of the porch. "Then he won't be our problem anymore."

Shock and disillusionment chilled her.

When she reached the grass, she turned to glare back up at him. "Did you have anything to do with getting him disinherited?"

Caleb Hamilton's bushy eyebrows shot up, the sun glinting off his sheriff's star. "Of course not. But I'll bet I know who did."

She waited. Curious. She might be angry with him for a lot of things, but there was no denying her father had his ear to the ground for happenings around Silent Spring. "Who?"

"Duke's other son, Clayton Reynolds, had a huge blow-up with him before he left town for good," her dad explained, leaning his elbows on the deck railing as he looked down at her. "I heard from more than one person that Clayton said he and Gavin would get even with their old man one day when they destroyed the legacy he'd groomed for his other two sons."

Frowning, she tried to make sense of that. "And you think Duke wrote Clayton and Gavin out of the will to ensure that didn't happen?"

Her dad shrugged, scrubbing a hand along the back of his neck. "He probably figured it would be better not

to chance it than to leave his estate to a pair of hooli-
gans who were only out to wreck it."

Indignation fired through her. "Gavin Kingsley is not
a 'hooligan.' He's a good person, Dad, and I'm disappointed that you were too busy holding an old grudge
to see that."

Her father opened his mouth as if to refute her or
make excuses, none of which she had the least interest in
hearing. Not when she didn't know how she could trust
a word he said. So she held up her hand, shook her head.

Pivoting fast, she stalked away, ignoring the sound
of him calling out her name, because she didn't want
to argue anymore today. Learning what she had about
her father hurt.

That's what she felt foremost.

And yet, as she slid into the driver's seat of her truck
and contemplated everything else that had come to light
today, she couldn't deny a tiny worry about Gavin. Or,
more to the point, about her feelings for Gavin.

Their night together had been nothing short of epic.

Not just because the sex had been blow-your-mind
amazing.

But because she'd woken in the middle of the night to
all kinds of feels. He'd taken her for a glider ride. He'd
wanted to show her the garden his mother made. He'd
held her during an anxiety attack and hadn't demanded
explanations later.

He'd even felt the scars on her shoulder and hadn't
pressed, giving her time to share her story when she
was ready.

Gavin had become special to her.

While that was exciting and gave her all kinds of butterflies, she also remembered that her father's distorted vision of him was based on at least a few shreds of evidence. Gavin had dated widely. He had a reputation for thrill seeking—both in life and love.

And no matter how much Lauryn had loved every minute of their night together, a part of her worried about Camille Jorgensen and all the other women who couldn't wait to bid on him at Studs for Sale. Her faith in her own judgment right now was shaky at best, considering what she'd just learned about her dad.

Gavin would be leaving town soon, as her father pointed out. So if she had feelings for him that needed resolving, she needed to do it soon because the bachelor auction was coming fast—just five days away now. And then Gavin would leave Silent Spring forever to start over somewhere else.

A thought that turned the butterfly feeling into a lead ball in her gut.

Twelve

Driving home from Wyoming after a day spent walking potential ranch properties, Gavin steered his truck toward the Hooves and Hearts Horse Rescue and the woman who had been on his mind nonstop since their passionate night together.

Since dropping her off at her house the day before, he'd tried to give her space. She'd been agitated after discovering the news about her father, so they hadn't spoken about where things stood between the two of them. Had it been wrong of him to share what he had about the sheriff?

The thought troubled him, along with the fear that he'd let things spiral out of control between them too quickly. As much as he'd wanted her—craved her— he'd known that acting on impulse when it came to their chemistry could have negative consequences, given their past.

He'd wanted that date with her to show her another side of himself. Instead, they'd ended up in bed together, and he worried that he'd proven all her original concerns about him. That he was a player and a ladies' man, a reputation from his bull-riding days that he hadn't done a damn thing to squash even though it was vastly overrated, since he'd been hell-bent to get under his father's skin.

Shortsighted of him now that he'd met a woman whose opinion really mattered.

She really mattered.

And that was the other thing that troubled him. What did he do about the growing feelings for Lauryn when he wasn't going to remain in Silent Spring even one day after that bachelor auction? The war with his father had died along with Duke Kingsley, but that didn't mean Gavin wanted any part of the complex network of businesses tied to the family name, let alone Kingsland Ranch.

At least he'd been able to share his point of view about that with his followers when he'd scheduled his spotlight post for the bachelor auction. He hadn't seen the reaction online yet, but he hoped once his fans knew it was his decision to part ways with the family businesses, they would halt the boycott efforts of Kingsley holdings. He'd hated seeing the Stockyard so empty, especially when Levi had started the place on his own.

Now, turning onto the back road that led to Lauryn's horse rescue, he admired the obvious hard work she'd put into the place. He recalled the property from years before, when it had been a hobby ranch for a family who fell on hard times. Gavin had been friends with the younger son, and could remember how overgrown it had been at the time.

Today, the access road had been paved and widened, brush cleared from both sides and symmetrical rows of ornamental trees planted. The effect was welcoming, and he had no doubt the horses entering the rescue appreciated the smoother ride to their new home.

Farther ahead, he could see the arched sign reading Hooves and Hearts. Six-foot brick columns held the wooden fence posts, wrought iron lamps on either side illuminating his way. Seeing what she was doing here, especially once he reached the spacious new stables she'd built, made him glad she'd talked him into staying through the bachelor auction. Her cause was a good one, and she would put the funds raised to truly worthwhile use.

He admired her work ethic, especially knowing that life had come easier for him, given his father's wealth. Even though he wanted to forge his own future going forward, he was still launching from a platform of support.

Pulling up to the stone ranch house with wide wooden porches, he parked in the driveway. He half wished he'd brought Rocco with him, as his dog adored Lauryn, and the Rottweiler would have fun exploring this place. But it wouldn't have been fair to the animal to be cooped up in the truck for the three-and-a-half-hour drive each way to view prospective ranches.

As he opened the truck door and stepped down to

the driveway, Lauryn appeared, silhouetted in the front entrance way.

His heart rate kicked up just seeing her.

Until, as he walked closer, the expression on her face became clearer. Her eyes were glistening. Her lower lip trembled.

Worry for her filled his chest as he quickened his step.

"Lauryn, what's wrong? Are you all right?" He slid a protective arm around her shoulders, feeling her warmth through the long gray sweater she wore over a Hooves and Hearts–logo T-shirt and black leggings.

A tiger-striped cat curled figure eights around her legs, offering feline comfort as they stood on the welcome mat under the glow of the porch light.

"I'm okay." She sniffed, swiping the sleeve of her sweater beneath her eyes. "The past few days have been a lot, after learning the truth about my dad and some other things he told me. And now today—"

A long, shaky sigh eased free as he held her.

"What about today?" he prompted, regretting that he'd shared something causing her pain.

She bit her lip for a long moment. Then, seeming to come to a decision, she nodded toward the porch swing swaying gently in the evening breeze.

"Let's sit," she suggested, sniffling once more, her eyes puffy. "I owed you an explanation anyway."

Confused, he moved with her toward the swing, holding the cedar bench seat steady for her while she took a seat on the thick blue cushion. Then he settled into the spot beside her.

"You don't need to share anything unless you want to," he reminded her, unwilling to pry even though he was curious.

Mostly, he just wanted to offer whatever comfort he could.

"But I told you that I would explain the anxiety attack, and I never did." Taking a deep breath, she relaxed against the planked seat, tipping her head onto his shoulder. "Today I want to share the story. I need to."

"Of course," he reassured her, stroking a stray strand of hair from her cheek. "I'm listening."

Around them, the evening grew cooler, so he pulled a spare fleece blanket from the back of the swing to drape over her legs. The scents of hay and earth from the stables and paddock nearby permeated the air. Every now and then, a whinny or a soft snort came from the barn area. The tiger-striped cat jumped onto the swing to take a seat on Lauryn's other side.

"I told you that, before the Hamiltons adopted me, I was in foster homes," she began, smoothing the blanket over her lap. "But I didn't tell you about the best friend I made in a group home where I lived for a couple of years. Jamie."

The careful way she said the name, with a wealth of emotion behind the word, made his gut clench for fear of where the story would end. He tucked her closer to his side, letting her speak without interrupting.

"She was a year older than me," Lauryn continued, her breath warm against his shirt where she rested against him. "Jamie liked all the same books I did, and we were happy kindred spirits in a house full of hard-

luck kids. The farmhouse was old and not well maintained, but our foster parents made some of the outer
buildings off-limits to keep us safe."

He felt colder by the minute as she spoke, so he
couldn't begin to imagine what the story was doing to
her. Tension clawed up the back of his neck, but he tried
not let it affect the way he held her.

Pausing, she placed a hand on his chest and levered
herself up a little so she could face him before she
continued. "But I was really drawn to one of them—
a dilapidated potting shed with a small porch—just a
step, really, and two columns in front of it." Her eyes
closed briefly as she dragged in a shuddering breath.
"And I talked Jamie into going in there with me one
day even though she thought it looked…unsafe." She bit
her lip. "She went in with me anyhow, and we started
reading *A Separate Peace*." Her voice failed her. She
swallowed hard. "There was a terrible cracking sound.
Like a tree falling. I looked up at her for a fraction of
an instant before the structure collapsed."

"Lauryn." Her name erupted from his lips on a
pained sound he hadn't meant to make. But he couldn't
imagine how awful that had been for her. "How badly
were you hurt?"

She shook her head impatiently. "It's not a story
about me. You felt the scars on my shoulder. What happened to me was nothing. I tried to get Jamie out, but—"

He waited, wishing she didn't have to say the next
words. But only because he hated that she'd lived them.

"—she didn't make it," Lauryn finished, exhaling a
long, slow breath. "She died because I convinced her

to be somewhere we shouldn't have been in the first place. If I'd listened to her—"

His stomach dropped as he reached for her, sick in his gut for what Lauryn had been through. She couldn't have been more than twelve at that time, and she'd had to grapple with something horrific all on her own.

"It wasn't your fault, Lauryn." He hugged her to him. Stroked a hand over her back. "You were a child. Both of you were. And you both deserved people looking out for your welfare."

"Logically, I know you're right," she admitted softly, her voice muffled against his shirt. "But it took a lot of years to let go of the guilt. And even now…it's an effort to remember that I shouldn't blame myself."

She pulled back from him, peering up into his eyes.

"I'm so sorry you went through that." He cupped her shoulders in his hands, rubbing along her arms. "So, so damned sorry. And I can't even imagine how much it upset you when those kids shook the tent poles in 4-H that day."

He hated that he'd been a part of that. Not that he'd done the shaking, but he'd been there when she'd turned and run. That day must have been an awful reminder for her.

"I didn't even remember the 4-H incident until you brought it up. It's odd that I blocked that episode out of my mind, but all these years later, I still remember exactly where we were in *A Separate Peace*."

"I would have never let them touch that tent pole if I'd known." It was a useless thing to say about a moment long past when she'd gone through something so much worse. But it was the only thing he'd had any control of in that time of her life.

"I know." A wobbly smile brightened her face briefly. "And living without her has been hard, but I've done it, year after year. It's just always tougher on this date, the anniversary of her death."

"Today?"

At her nod of confirmation, he pulled her into his arms, holding her tight. He'd read somewhere once that a hug helped someone hurt or grieving because it gave a boundary to pain, enclosing it. He didn't know if that was true for how Lauryn felt now, but he hoped so.

He'd do anything to ease her hurt. Needed to do more for this woman who gave so much of herself to help others.

Which gave him an idea.

Easing away from her, he tipped her chin up so he could see into her eyes. "We could have a bonfire." He'd noticed a firepit when he'd dropped her off here before. "And make it like a memorial in her honor."

Something shifted in her gaze. Something that looked almost…hopeful.

Straightening, he warmed to the idea, remembering a similar gesture his mother had made for him a long time ago, when they'd said a formal goodbye to their old life as full-time residents of Kingsland Ranch. "I don't know if it would help, but you could even write a letter to her—"

"—and let the fire carry the ashes of my words to her." Lauryn finished the sentence her own way, already nodding. "Yes, Gavin. I would really like that."

* * *

An hour later, Lauryn sat beside Gavin at the roaring blaze he'd built to commemorate Jamie.

He'd pulled over a patio bench from her back deck so they could sit beside each other while she penned her letter on a notepad lit by the orange flames inside the stone-rimmed pit. Her legs were curled beneath her as she worked. She'd put her cat, Festus, in the house earlier so she wouldn't have to try finding him in the dark. Night birds called to one another, their whistles and songs audible over the crackling of the logs and hiss of sparks that made their way onto the cool, damp grass.

Even the act of writing the letter felt therapeutic, reminding her of the days at equine therapy. Gavin had been wise to suggest the exercise. And the fire itself.

Both comforted her in a way she'd really needed today.

For now, she'd put aside the other worries about her father, about her parents' marriage. About Gavin himself and what would happen after the bachelor auction. She simply concentrated on her lost foster sister, the grief and the love still overflowing her heart.

"I'm finished with my letter now." She stared down at the pages on her legal pad. The reminiscences about stories they'd shared—those they'd read and those they'd told one another about their lives. Details she hadn't shared with another soul since.

"Your hands must be cold," he observed, his brown eyes full of concern and tenderness.

She appreciated him being here so much.

"They're fine." Still, she pressed the back of her

knuckles to her cheek to warm them. "And I'm glad I wrote it all out."

He withdrew a folded sheet of paper from the pocket of his jacket. All this time, he'd been dressed in a gray suit and dark blue dress shirt. She knew he'd been touring ranch properties across the border today, and he looked every inch the high-powered rancher.

"I hope you don't mind if I—" He closed his hand again. Crumpling the paper a bit. He cleared his throat and began once more. "I wrote my own goodbye just now. This one is a bit overdue as well."

His father? If it was Duke Kingsley he had in mind, that seemed like a good thing. She recognized Gavin had been deeply hurt by the disinheritance and hoped maybe this would help give him closure.

She took his free hand in hers and squeezed it tight. "Of course I don't mind."

They stood shoulder to shoulder for a long moment, staring into the yellow and red flames flickering upward.

"Are you ready?" Gavin held out his paper toward the pit, the firelight casting shadows over his handsome face.

"I am." Folding the pages of her letter, she kissed the missive and tossed it into the hungry inferno.

She watched as the paper curled and turned black. Shrinking and then disintegrating. Sending a few white ashes out into the spring wind.

Beside her, she felt Gavin pitch his letter into the fire a moment afterward. She closed her eyes, letting the moment wash over her. The grief and the goodbye, the love and the remembering. Her heart felt full, but in a good way. Or at least, a better way.

"Thank you for this." Her voice sounded scratchy from the emotions in her throat.

"I'm glad I could be here with you today."

Turning toward him, seeing the strength and warmth of his big body beside her, she felt a rush of hunger for him. Need.

He reached toward her, thumbing aside a tear she hadn't realized was on her cheek. His touch sent a shiver through her.

Not questioning the impulse, she captured his wrist and held his hand to her face, kissing his palm.

"I'm glad you were here, too, because I'm not done needing you tonight." She stepped closer until they were chest to chest, breathing one another's air. "If I put out this blaze, will you come in the house and start another one with me?"

"I want that. So much, Lauryn, I want that." In spite of his words, he didn't move. He remained very, very still. "But I don't want to take advantage of a vulnerable time—"

"You won't be," she urged him, laying both hands on his chest. Smoothing her way down his shirt front. "How is it taking advantage of me when I'm doing the asking? I just want to lose myself. Forget about everything else."

His hands gripped her hips. To halt her? Or to pull her nearer?

She held her breath while she waited to find out, her

breath coming faster as she remembered the taste of his kisses. The feel of his mouth all over her body.

Maybe her thoughts showed in her eyes, because a moment later, he was kissing her like his life depended on it. Hungrily. Demanding.

And she answered him with her whole body, pressing shamelessly to him, rocking closer still. Her hands worked under his jacket to splay over the broad muscles of his shoulders until he jerked back.

"I'll take care of the fire," he announced, already moving toward the hose she'd laid out when they first began laying the logs in the pit. "You should go inside and warm up."

Switching on the water, he sprayed down the flames so they smoked and hissed.

"I'll wait and warm up with you." She grabbed a bucket of dirt she kept nearby and added that to the pit, smothering the remaining fire.

He'd already made things better with the bonfire and his physical presence and his compassionate ear. Surely if she lost herself in the chemistry of their attraction, she would be able to burn away the rest of the feelings buzzing all through her.

Gavin shut off the hose and took her by the hand, the determined expression on his face sending a thrill of anticipation through her in spite of all the heavy feelings of the day. She needed this. Desperately.

Needed him.

Minutes later, they were in her dark kitchen, kissing their way through the house and bumping into things, unable to let one another go long enough to switch on a light. She toed off her shoes and then tripped on them, all without letting go of Gavin.

"Where is your bedroom?" he asked when he released her lips long enough to lick a path along her neck.

"Left," she murmured, her legs already trembling from that wicked glide of his tongue over her throat. "We're close."

She tried to guide them, but his hands sliding up under her shirt distracted her. Her skin tingled. She backed them into the hallway wall before righting their path.

Maybe his eyes had adjusted then, because he lifted her up and carried her the rest of the way, elbowing closed the door behind them. Her bedside alarm had a blue light around the base, enough to see once they were inside. She peeled off her cardigan and tee with zero finesse, unsteady on her feet.

"Lauryn." His voice halted her briefly, and she paused in unhooking her bra to see his eyes fastened to her body. "Let me."

Awareness stirred in her belly. Lower. But she forced her arms down to her side while he closed the distance between them, his shirt and jacket already discarded. Then she couldn't think anymore because his mouth found her nipple, licking his way around the peak before drawing on it. Her back arched, sensations spiraling to all corners of her body from that hot kiss.

He unhooked her bra and slipped it off her before giving her other breast the same attention. She reached to unfasten his belt and found his hand already there, working the clasp and placket before he stepped out of his pants.

"Do you have a condom?" She had purchased some just in case after their time together at the mountain retreat, but retrieving them from the bathroom would delay what she wanted—needed—most.

"Yes, here. You hold on to it." He passed the packet to her a moment before he picked her up and laid her on the bed.

She was tearing it open when he dragged off her leggings and panties. A moment later, he covered her and she rolled the condom into place. Briefly, their eyes met. Held.

His heart pounded so hard she felt it in her chest. She laid her hand over the place where it thumped, and all the feelings she'd been battling today threatened to come to the surface.

When he edged his way inside her, she welcomed the rush of heat and hunger for him, her body ready for how good he could make her feel. He moved slowly at first, giving her time to savor every inch of him. She nipped his shoulder, her fingernails lightly pressing into his skin.

"You feel too good," he whispered hoarsely in her ear, his hips rocking harder.

Faster.

"You feel better," she whispered back, the promise of her release already balling tight in her midsection. Her spine arched as she pressed herself into him, meeting every thrust.

When he reached between them to apply pressure

exactly where she needed it, pleasure unraveled in wave after delicious wave, her body clenching his tight.

Gavin rocked his hips harder. Deeper. His shout vibrated through her as he found his finish.

Fulfillment. Contentment. She breathed them in and out with every breath for long moments afterward, his body a hot weight that she welcomed where he slumped against her. The night had been special in so many ways.

He slid to one side of her, tugging a blanket off the footboard to wrap around them. Cocooning them together. The movement must have dislodged her cat from somewhere along the foot of her bed, Festus mewing softly before leaping to sit on a windowsill.

Gavin stroked a hand over her hair for a few minutes before his fingers slid lower, down her shoulder to the place where her network of scars lay. He traced the lines carefully, outlining each ropey layer. "Are you okay?"

She understood what he was asking. Recalled his concern about indulging their intimacy, so new and untested, on a difficult anniversary day for her.

"I am. And I'm glad you're here." For a moment, she allowed the peaceful feeling she'd experienced by the bonfire to fill her up again, savoring the knowledge that she'd remembered her friend—her family—in a positive way.

But thinking about the family she'd made for herself as a foster child called to mind Gavin's fractured family. She needed to share what her father had told her about the disinheritance, and she wasn't quite sure how to bring it up without causing him pain.

"How about you?" she asked, thinking back to the note he'd tossed into the fire. "Did the letter bring you any closure?"

"I was glad I got a few things off my chest," he admitted, though something about the way he'd phrased it made her think there was a wealth of sentiment behind the simple words.

She wished the room were brighter so she could read the nuances of his expression more clearly. Stroking her fingertips up his arm, she remained quiet, hoping he'd share more.

"I just wish I understood why my father cut me off." He gave her a speculative look. "One of the reasons I agreed to stay for the bachelor auction was because I thought you might know since you worked with him."

"Me?" Elbowing up higher to face him, indignation chilled her insides. "You wanted to get close to me to find out how much I knew?"

He swallowed hard but met her eyes. "At first, yes."

Disappointment threatened to swallow her whole. All that attraction— had it been a lie?

But Gavin didn't seem to notice how his words gutted her. He rushed to add, "Then I got to know you, and I realized you wouldn't have hid something like that from me if you'd known Duke's reasons."

Small consolation for being doubted. For being… used for his own ends?

She turned that over in her mind, telling herself that her emotions were too raw right now to see the situation clearly. Still, it stung.

Gavin's attention had drifted to the ceiling as he

lay beside her, seemingly deep in thought. "Anyway, I knew I wasn't his favorite, but I never knew he resented me to that point where he'd exclude me from everything related to the Kingsley legacy…except the name itself." He gave a harsh laugh. "Clayton should be glad he wasn't saddled with the moniker, when our father planned to rip away everything it stood for."

Shoving aside her own hurts, Lauryn could understand Gavin's pain. Shunning two of his sons hadn't been fair of Duke Kingsley, but she also knew that bitterness and resentment festered worse than any physical wound.

As sad and disillusioned as she felt with her own father, she also knew she would work to forgive him because they were family.

"I asked Dad if he knew anything about the disinheritance when I confronted him about working for Duke," she ventured carefully, hoping the information would at least give him some peace.

"And?" Gavin sat up, his shoulders tense.

Lauryn turned to flick the bedside lamp on low, needing to see him better. Wanting to be diplomatic with what she had to share. "Dad heard Clayton and your father had a huge falling out before Clayton left Silent Spring—"

"That's hardly a secret." Gavin's forehead furrowed as he scowled. "We're still searching for him because he's fallen off the grid."

Placing a hand on his arm, she hoped the touch would gentle a harsh fact. "My father said people heard Clayton threaten to get even with Duke one day when he and you destroyed the legacy he'd built for his other two sons."

Gavin's brows shot up. "That I hadn't heard, though it doesn't surprise me. And the sheriff thinks Duke cut us out to try and protect what he'd worked hard to build." Frowning, Gavin shook his head as he seemed to weigh the possibility of his father cutting him off because he feared the Kingsley legacy would be run into the ground at Gavin's hands. "My own father didn't understand a single damned thing about me if he believed that."

"But doesn't that make you rethink leaving Silent Spring? If your father was only trying to protect his assets—"

"From his own sons?" he interrupted sharply, turning to find his shirt and punching into the sleeves. "No matter his reasons, disinheriting tells the world that either he didn't trust us or he didn't love us. I'm not about to stick around a town where everyone thinks I wasn't worthy of my old man."

Was Gavin leaving now? His abruptness caught her by surprise.

She understood he was upset, but she wasn't sure what to think about an abrupt departure after what they'd just shared. Still, she slid from the bed to find her long cardigan and slipped it on. The gray cashmere covered her like a robe, the soft fabric providing scant comfort when the conversation was an unhappy one.

"Why would anyone think that?" She didn't think the argument about not being "worthy" held any water. Gavin had carved out an identity separate from his father's, and he'd been successful in bull riding and ranching without any Kingsley family assistance. "Duke Kingsley had a mercurial temper, and everyone in his life knew it. Just because he made a bad judgment call with his will doesn't mean you have to turn your back on your brothers. They're your family."

While she spoke, Gavin had finished dressing, although his shirt remained half-buttoned and his jacket lay on the bed between them. She paced circles around her side of the bed, telling herself they weren't arguing. And yet, with the whole bed between them, their tense postures and the anxiety balling in her stomach, the moment felt combustible. Like it could turn into an argument quickly if she wasn't careful.

Was she pushing him away to make it easier when he inevitably left her? She hadn't meant to do that, but here they were. Her heart pounded harder, confusion and her feelings for him twisting into knots.

"Not according to my father, we're not," Gavin reminded her, his eyes dark with the grudge he now bore.

Frustration swelled. "How can you allow him to decide who is important in your life and who isn't? Your brothers love you and want you to remain in town to build the business you agreed to run together."

"Or they could just feel guilty about Duke's decision, and they're offering to cut Clayton and me in so they feel better about themselves." He spread his arms wide, exasperated. "I'm not going to take pity handouts from an estate that was not intended for me. I'm not some charity case for them to swoop in and save."

Her frustration turned to red-hot anger at his words.

She threw the blanket back on the bed in a frustrated toss, her other hand clenched tighter where she held her sweater closed.

"Do you see it as a 'pity handout' to offer someone a sense of love and family?" Her pulse hammered an angry tattoo, her blood heating. "Do you think I'm a charity case, too, because my parents gave me a home when they took in an abandoned kid?"

He swiped a hand across his face, which had gone a shade paler. "Lauryn, no. Of course that's not what I meant."

But the dam on the emotions roiling inside her on this day had burst. Yes, she'd found new healing on the anniversary of Jamie's death. That hadn't soothed the new ache of her father's betrayal of her trust or made her feel any better about her parents' marriage. Or the fact that Gavin had only initiated a relationship with her to find out what she knew about Duke's will. Oh, and add to that the fact that Gavin couldn't shake the dust of Silent Spring off his expensive shoes quickly enough, and she had the perfect recipe for stress. Tension. Unease.

And now? The stress ball had exploded into messy shards that scattergun-shot all around her.

"No matter how much you resent your father, Gavin, you were still the indulged son of a Kingsley for the first ten years of your life. You knew luxury and security that most people never experience." She wondered if he could even imagine the kinds of places she'd lived before finding a permanent home with the Hamiltons. "I understand if you want to walk away from the money.

But I will never comprehend how you can throw away people who want to call you *brother* and claim you as one of their own."

He rounded the bed to stand closer to her, perhaps to argue the point more, but she didn't think she was in a good position to talk any more about a stance she viewed as stubborn. Arrogant, even. Yes, her perspective might be different from other people's because of how she was raised. Because she'd lost a foster sister in a blink, and she'd never have that piece of her heart and her family back again.

Even the sheriff, for all his flaws, wasn't someone she would give up on without a fight. Just as her dad hadn't given up on her, even when they disagreed. Family mattered.

"Lauryn, please. I never meant to suggest my brothers were expendable. In time, maybe we'll work things out."

She nodded, her mouth tight. "Maybe you will. I hope you have enough time to do that. But since you're going to be leaving after the bachelor auction anyway, maybe it's just as well we move on too."

In her heart, she knew she was the expendable one to him.

And maybe that was the stressor that had been hurting most of all tonight. No matter how amazing their time together had been, Gavin would walk away from her without a backward glance once their expiration date arrived.

He even confirmed it for her when he gave a nod a moment later.

Agreeing with her that moving on would be best.

Soon, she stood alone in her darkened bedroom. As the deeper pain of what had just happened began to sink in, Lauryn realized she had just said goodbye to the man with whom she'd fallen in love. Of course, she'd had to do it since he hadn't wanted her for more than a fling.

She'd even fooled herself at some point that was all she wanted too. But with the pain of losing him spreading to every atom in her body, she began to see how very wrong she had been.

Thirteen

Gavin drove to the Stockyard.

The bar would be closing soon, but he wasn't in need of a drink after his talk with Lauryn that had gone so devastatingly wrong. No, his thoughts were already fractured and pinballing around his mind so fast that his head spun like he'd had a few too many as it was.

What he needed right now was his brother and the reality check that only Levi Kingsley could provide. Well, that and a little company from his dog. Gavin dug his fingers into the thick black fur of Rocco's ruff as the Rottweiler mix sat beside him on the front seat, his lead secured for safety. Gavin had made a stop at the house to see the dog since he'd left the Rotty alone for most of the day. They'd taken a walk together, then Rocco had jumped in the truck cab for this late night errand.

Now, cracking the window of the truck for the dog and assuring Rocco he'd be back out in a few minutes, Gavin parked his truck in the near-empty lot of the bar, close enough to the front that he'd be able to keep an eye on his pet. This wouldn't take long anyhow. He charged across the gravel, up the steps and through the door, wondering why the former hot spot was still so vacant. He should ask Levi about that. See what he could do to help business.

Except the first words out of his mouth when he saw Levi seated at the end of the bar were purely selfish because what weighed on his mind more than anything else was Lauryn.

"Does it seem like I'm turning my back on you and Quinton to pull up stakes here and move to Wyoming?" he blurted, dropping into a seat two down from Levi. He and his brother were the only people in the place except for a couple of regulars sharing a drink at the other end. "Or does it take the pressure off, knowing you don't have to rework the whole estate to try and divvy it up more?"

"Good evening to you too," Levi greeted him dryly, not turning away from his electronic tablet, where he was working on a spreadsheet of some kind.

"Right. Sorry to abandon manners in a time of personal crisis, but I'm in serious need of wise perspective, and you're one of the most grounded guys I know." Raking a hand through his hair, he couldn't believe he'd been in Lauryn's bed just an hour before.

Happier than he could remember being in a long, long time.

Until a simple discussion turned into an argument

that he'd been completely unprepared for. How had he misstepped so badly?

Shutting down the tablet screen, Levi turned weary eyes his way. "I wouldn't be so sure about that. Maybe I just play the role of responsible firstborn because that's what was expected of me."

Something in his brother's tone was off. A darkness that he didn't normally associate with Levi. Remembering what Lauryn had said about hoping he'd have time to work things out with his brothers if he left town, a pang shot through him.

"You're right. It's wrong to always expect you to hold things together. It wasn't fair of Dad, and it's not fair of me either." He slid his elbows on the bar and dropped his head into his hands. He didn't want to have any traits in common with Duke Kingsley, but he was beginning to see a selfish streak that he didn't care for. Straightening again, he turned back to his brother. "But maybe that's all the more reason I'd like an answer to my question. Is it selfish of me to leave town? To leave you and Quinton to enjoy the inheritance?"

"Loaded question, brother." Levi reached behind the bar for a large jug of water and a second glass. He topped off his and then poured the second full for Gavin while the jukebox played a sorrowful country song that echoed the bar's dejected atmosphere.

"But considering Lauryn just as good as called me a self-centered ass when she booted me out of her house tonight—" damn, but it hurt to remember the way she'd told him they needed to move on "—could you do me a favor and still answer my question?"

Levi studied him over the rim of his glass for a moment before he set it back on the bar. "Is it selfish to follow your own path? Of course not. Do I wish you could wait until we settle the public relations nightmare Dad created when he severed the family in half? Yeah, Gav. I really do."

The mirror up to his actions was necessary. But that didn't mean he liked what he saw.

Swearing softly, Gavin drained the water glass.

"You've told me that too. I guess I just didn't believe it before because I couldn't imagine why you'd want me hanging around when eventually you'd need to cut me loose." He still didn't quite understand it.

Levi and Quinton had worked their asses off to be where they were today. That their father left them everything he'd worked for as well wasn't their fault. Duke Kingsley had manipulated them all with his power play from the grave intended to divide the family.

A dark scowl descended over his brother's features. "What you don't seem to appreciate is that I literally cannot do this—I don't *want* to do this—without you. If you choose to walk away from the other business interests, it would be one thing. A PR nightmare, but I'd deal with it." Levi waved good-night to one of the regulars who stood up to leave the bar. "It's one thing to break up the business, but I don't want this to break up the family. Don't let this drive a wedge between us."

Gavin recalled how many times he'd turned to his brothers for help and advice. Like tonight. When he'd been out of his head with fear about losing Lauryn, his first move had been to seek out his sibling. Maybe he needed to think more about what he'd be leaving behind if he went through with his plans to relocate. Did he want to alienate Quinton and Levi? Not to mention Clayton, if the guy ever turned up again?

While he mulled over his brother's words, Levi asked, "So you and Lauryn Hamilton?"

Memories of her smile after their glider ride reminded him of how much they'd had together. They'd grown close quickly, but their time had been significant. Meaningful.

She'd let him hold her last night when she was hurt and grieving. He'd been grateful as hell that his presence had comforted her.

"Yeah. Me and Lauryn." He shut his eyes, picturing her face when she'd asked him to leave. "I didn't see it coming, didn't know how different she would be from anyone I've ever dated."

Levi snorted. "With all due respect to your past girlfriends, you should have come to your wise and grounded older brother for some perspective before now, and I would have told you that Lauryn is nothing like the Camille Jorgensens of the world."

He could acknowledge he'd kept relationships superficial in the past. Maybe it had something to do with how complicated relationships had been in his family. His MO in the past had been to cut and run before things got messy. Sort of like he'd been planning to run from his brothers to avoid the aftermath of the disinheritance wrecking ball. For that matter, he'd been dangerously close to running from Lauryn—the best thing to ever happen to him.

Maybe it all looked more obvious in hindsight. Or maybe Levi had a point, and Gavin simply hadn't been ready to date someone like Lauryn before now. Hell, based on the way she'd tossed him out on his ear, maybe he still wasn't ready.

But he realized now without a single doubt that he wanted to be. Because what he felt for any woman before Lauryn couldn't compare with how deep his emotions ran for her already, even though their relationship was new.

It was special.

More than that, actually. He loved Lauryn.

Lauryn, who worked tirelessly to support a cause that mattered to her deeply. Lauryn, who—unlike him—had always strived to make good choices. She'd survived a traumatic past and fashioned a life for herself that was honest and true. Her goodness humbled him. And he wanted to be the kind of man who deserved a woman like that.

"You're right." Scrubbing a hand along his jaw, Gavin let the truth wash over him, infusing him with new purpose. New understanding. "I can't leave Montana because I won't leave Lauryn." Rapping his knuckles on the bar, he got to his feet, knowing he needed to figure out something fast. Make big plans before the bachelor auction. Because Lauryn deserved everything he had to give. "I love her."

A grin stole over Levi's face as he raised his water glass in a silent toast. "I knew I liked that woman."

Gavin was already backing away, a hundred possibilities spinning through his mind for how to show her how much he cared. How he could be a person who deserved her.

Still, he paused to point a finger in Levi's direction, acknowledging his help. "Thank you for this. For everything. I'm going to be a better brother."

"I'm holding you to it," Levi called back, but Gavin was already jogging out the door to his truck.

He had a one-in-a-million woman to win back.

Circling the Studs for Sale event with her tablet in hand, Lauryn ran through her checklist for tasks that needed to be completed before the bachelor auction got underway. She'd clung to her lists like a lifeline for the past two days since things ended with Gavin, relying on nonstop activity to prevent herself from thinking about him.

Regretting words spoken in haste before he left Silent Spring for good.

"Champagne?" A tuxedoed young server stopped in front of her with a tray full of bubbling flutes.

"None for me, thank you." Lauryn waved the server on, glancing around the event inside the Kingsland Ranch Thoroughbred-show arena, temporarily transformed into an elegant black-tie venue.

Of course, considering the state-of-the-art facility built to Duke Kingsley's exacting specifications shortly before his death, it hadn't been difficult to decorate. The pale wood interior had a skylight that ran along the ridged roof, while laminated-timber trusses supported a curved ceiling.

Since the sun had set before the start of the evening

event, the skylight didn't help illuminate the arena, but the impressive stars of Big Sky Country were visible through the glass overhead. A popular country band that Gavin had secured for her played on the far end of the arena, the dance floor already filled with two-stepping couples. She saw her friends on the floor. Kendra and Hope danced together, their very different red gowns making them an eye-catching pair. Kendra wore a satin sheath with zero ornamentation, while Hope rocked a fringe-filled flapper-style dress. Lauryn had said hello to them briefly but hadn't had time to visit. She hoped they knew how much she appreciated their support.

Lauryn and her team of volunteers had decorated with red roses in heart-shaped wreaths, while an art gallery from Billings had brought an installation of ironworks sculptures from a Montana artist who worked with recycled horseshoes. The effect of the tall black-iron sculptures and wealth of red-rose wreaths was particularly lovely next to the backdrop of pale wood walls and columns of the arena. White lights and horseshoe table centerpieces completed the look while letting the custom architecture shine.

A familiar male voice sounded behind her. "Looks like your event will be quite a success."

"Dad?" she turned in surprise, seeing her parents dressed in their evening finery. A simple gray suit for him. A pretty purple wrap dress for her mother.

Her parents had RSVP'd—finally—the day before the event. But even then, she hadn't been certain whether or not they would attend. Her shoulders tensed as she faced her father.

Yet it was her mom who spoke first. "You look beautiful, darling." Violet leaned closer to kiss her cheek, and whispered, "Just hear your father out, okay?"

She nodded a bit woodenly, unsure what to expect since she'd wanted to hammer out their opposition to Gavin and her event long before now when she needed to focus on things running smoothly. But when her mom excused herself so that Lauryn and her father could speak privately, she refocused her attention on him. Just to hear him out, as her mom had asked.

Nearby, in the whirl of dancing couples, there were plenty of cowboy boots and Stetsons with tuxes given the Hooves and Hearts theme, the party well underway. It would be time for the auction soon, but she could spare her dad a few minutes.

"Lauryn, I just wanted to say I'm sorry for being so mule-headed about Gavin." Her father's blue eyes met hers. Even in the lowered lighting, she could see the emotions there. Sadness, maybe. Regret, even?

Some of her tension eased at her dad's overture. She knew making an effort wasn't easy.

"He's a better man than you realize," she told him quietly, her own regrets filling her chest, making her ache.

"Maybe you're right. But even if turns out that you aren't, I realized that an old grudge isn't worth losing you. You're too important to me."

Her throat clogged with emotion. The words soothing raw parts inside her. For the moment, the rest of the party disappeared while she looked into the eyes of a man who—she knew without question—had done his best to be a good father the only way he knew how.

"You're important to me too, Dad."

The corners of his mouth lifted. "Our talk made me realize that I've been a damned fool holding onto the past. I love your mother, and I'm lucky to have her." His blue eyes glanced away, searching the party.

Settling on Violet Hamilton where she shared a laugh with a friend near the dessert bar.

Lauryn's heart filled with relief. Gratitude that her dad could recognize what he had in his wife.

"I hope you make sure Mom knows that," she pressed, thinking how much her mother deserved an ardent, devoted partner who valued her.

"I promise I will." The other side of her dad's mouth curled in a full smile now. "And I'm going to make peace with Gavin Kingsley too. He's next on my list tonight."

"Really?" That surprised her more than anything else her father said.

And why did her heart have to go and start beating double time at just the mention of Gavin's name?

"It's never too late to admit a wrong." He settled his hands on Lauryn's shoulders and squeezed. "Are we okay though, you and me?"

"We're really good," she told him, meaning it. "Thank you for coming tonight."

Her dad wrapped her in a bear hug. "I'm so proud of you."

When he left her to seek out Violet again, a swell of

contentment filled her. She felt sure her father would heal things. Already, she felt better about where they stood.

If only the rest of her hurts were as easily remedied. Now, the scents of roses and treats from the dessert bar sweetened the air. She only wished she could share her satisfaction in the event with Gavin since he'd helped her with so much of the planning. The reason they had a packed house tonight was because of him. She'd received dozens of last-minute ticket requests during the week of the bachelor social media profiles.

No surprise, the most tickets were purchased on-line the day his profile ran. Her chest squeezed around a hollow ache at the knowledge that she'd pushed him away with both hands. She'd been scared of what she'd been feeling because falling in love with Gavin had seemed too risky.

Trusting others? Easier said than done after her birth parents had abandoned her, the foster home shuffles and loss of her foster sister. Even the rocky assimilation into her forever family. Stepping outside her comfort zone was hard as hell.

Thinking back on it now, she was all the angrier with herself when she should have been trying to embrace life and live hers to the fullest. Yet when it came to the biggest risk of all, she'd failed to take a chance.

Aggravated and hurt, she needed to return to her checklist before she wound up in tears again. This night was bigger than her feelings, although it wasn't easy to remember when every part of her ached.

As she returned her attention to the tablet, however, Levi Kingsley approached her. He'd been her official host for the evening since Gavin had pulled his support from all things related to the Kingsland Ranch.

"Lauryn, can you spare a moment?" Levi wore his traditional tuxedo with the ease of someone who had been born to wealth and privilege.

Whereas her dad would have rented his clothes for the evening, Lauryn recognized Levi's garb had been custom-tailored. Gavin's would be, too, she knew, though she hadn't seen him yet this evening. Several of the bachelors had opted to wait to make their appearance until the auction, which would begin soon. The auctioneer had already texted that she was taking the stage in five minutes.

"Certainly, I can," Lauryn answered, greeting Levi with a polite smile. "The auction doesn't start for a couple of minutes."

He passed her a white envelope with her name scrawled across the front in a bold, familiar hand. "Gavin asked me to give this to you before the auction."

Her heartbeat stuttered as she stared at the high-quality stationery, curious what Gavin could have to say to her in a note.

She didn't realize that she hadn't reached to take the paper until Levi actively pressed it into her palm.

"I hope you will read it upon receipt, Lauryn." Levi spoke quietly, in a tone meant for her ears alone. "I do believe it's very important to my brother. And, because of that, it's quite important to me as well."

Surprised at his words, when she had thought Levi would be angry with Gavin for leaving Montana and forsaking the business they'd planned together, she didn't know quite how to answer. But it didn't matter because Levi moved away again, leaving her a moment alone before the auction started to open the message.

Jitters swirled in her stomach as she slid a finger under the seal and tore open the envelope. Inside, there were two pieces of paper. One was a handwritten letter. The other a blank check signed by Gavin.

Confused, she ducked behind one of the horseshoe sculptures to gain a little privacy while she read.

You're the only woman in the world who matters to me.

The shocking opening line of the letter made her palm go to her chest. She pressed it against the bodice of her crystal-embellished silk crepe de chine gown, needing a hand there to soothe the erratic pulse that hammered hard in answer.

The idea of a date with anyone else—even for one evening—is something I can't bear when my heart craves you alone. I will cover your bid of any amount, but I'm asking you—no, pleading with you—to win me at the bachelor auction. I promise you, whether you choose to bid on me or not, I will not leave Montana. More importantly, I will never leave you if you opt to give me another chance.

Yours Forever, Gavin

By the time she reached the end of the note, her hand had moved from her pounding heart to her lips, where she needed to stifle a gasp of surprise and emotion.

He wrote almost as if…he loved her too?

Stuffing down the swell of hope at the possibility, Lauryn hurried to the coat check table in the back, where she'd left her purse. She didn't have time to over-think this, not when the time was fast approaching to place her bid for Gavin. Already, the auctioneer was taking the stage, announcing the start of the event and introducing the first bachelor.

After requesting her bag, she tucked the letter and the check inside the beaded silk before handing off her tablet to an event volunteer. She couldn't possibly be responsible for organizing anything else tonight when her thoughts were in a tangle with Gavin Kingsley at the center, her heart racing faster than any Thorough-bred's at a finish line.

She needed girlfriend support to get through the auction before Gavin came on stage.

"Excuse me," she murmured as she made her way through the crowd that had gathered around the stage near the band.

A small runway had been erected in front of the stage so the bachelors could walk closer to the people bidding on them—a blend of men and women since the bachelors had been able to invite bids from whatever gender preference they chose.

"Lauryn," a woman's voice whispered as she neared the stage.

Turning, she found Ellen and Chip Crawford, her

former foster parents, arm in arm. Pausing to hug them both, she soaked up the love and support from people who would always be family in her eyes. "I'm so glad you're here. Thank you for coming."

"We wouldn't have missed it for the world," Ellen exclaimed animatedly even though she still kept her voice quiet in deference to the bidding war going on around them for the first bachelor. "And we won't keep you but wanted you to know that Zara is in love with Toffee. I've just been overjoyed to see their bond grow so quickly."

Her throat closed at the lump of emotion. This was why she'd worked so hard to grow Hooves and Hearts.

"Thank you for telling me that," she said once she'd cleared her throat. "You and Zara should come by the stables once I get the equine-therapy piece of the rescue up and running. I'll bet she'd enjoy meeting all the horses."

After agreeing to do just that, Ellen and Chip excused themselves, leaving Lauryn free to move closer to the stage again. She reached her friends, Hope and Kendra, to stand between them while bachelor after bachelor took the stage.

None of them Gavin.

Lauryn knew she'd slated him to go near the end of the line since he promised to start a huge bidding war. The prices women had bandied about on social media were astonishing, but she'd told herself that was just chatter and wouldn't be what she'd really receive in donations to Hooves and Hearts.

And how could she justify spending so much of Gavin's money if she were to outbid them all?

Because yes, she really, really wanted to do just that, and his letter made it clear he wanted that—wanted her—as well.

As another bachelor was awarded to a giddy lady surgeon from Billings for an astronomical price, Kendra leaned closer to observe quietly, "Lauryn, I'm so happy for you. The bids are going to be so great for the rescue."

Hope leaned in from Kendra's other side to add, "Now if only we could get Kendra to bid."

Kendra shook her head, her elegant blond updo sparkling from a spray of crystal flowers woven through the chignon. "I'm off the market, remember? Although, Lauryn, if I could afford it, I'd be bidding, too, even if I decidedly don't want to date anyone."

Squeezing Kendra's hand, Lauryn wanted to reassure her friends. "I'm just glad you're here. That's all the support I need." Biting her lip, she let go of Kendra's hand to reach in her purse. Withdrawing Gavin's letter, she passed it to her friends. "Okay, maybe I could use just a little more support. Tell me what you think I should do about this."

She watched as Kendra's eyes went wide. A moment later, so did Hope's.

"Is it wrong to bid his money?" she asked nervously, wondering what they were thinking. "I don't know if—"

"Are you insane?" Kendra whisper-hissed back at her as she turned to squeeze both of Lauryn's shoulders. "You have to go for it. This is the single most romantic thing I've ever heard of."

Bolstered by her friend's words, she started to smile even before Hope added, "You can't leave a man in love to the single-lady vultures, Lauryn. You have to win him."

Was he? A man in love?

Lauryn's heart curled possessively around the word, longing for it to be true. And winning this bid would offer an amazing first step in giving them time to explore their feelings.

The auctioneer's voice returned to the microphone then, her next announcement the one Lauryn had been waiting for. "And now, for our next bachelor. The one. The only. Your local bull-riding hero and stud expert, Gavin Kingsley."

The clamor that went up from the crowd might have intimidated Lauryn a week ago since it was blatantly obvious there was plenty of competition for Gavin's affections. And yet, as the man she wanted to see most in the world walked out onto the stage in his black bespoke tux, she couldn't doubt for an instant that he wanted only her.

His brown eyes lasered in on her, finding her in the throng and communicating everything she needed to know.

His feelings for her were still there. Focused fully and completely on her. The connection reaching out as tangibly as if he'd gathered her in his arms.

He didn't want to lose her any more than she wanted to lose him.

And the spark between them was more than alive and well. It was a fire that wouldn't go out.

Beside her, her friends were encouraging her as the bidding started, but she wasn't ready to show her hand just yet. Not that she wanted Gavin to wonder if she was going to bid on him. She guessed that he could see right through to her heart the same way she'd read his when he walked down the runway.

But they'd spent hours and hours planning this auction event together, and she wasn't about to let her prize stud go for any less than he deserved. Gavin Kingsley held a worth greater than she'd given him credit for. He was so much more than a handsome bull rider. So much more than a successful rancher.

Everything she needed to know about him she'd seen the day he'd held her through an anxiety attack. And again the night he'd helped her start a memorial blaze for her foster sister.

"Bid soon," Kendra urged her as the crowd quieted for the bidding war between two determined competitors. "They're already higher than any of the other bachelors."

Turning around to scout out the competing bidders, Lauryn recognized Camille Jorgensen as one of them. The other woman was a petite brunette in a beaded blue sari.

The auctioneer waited for a bid to top Camille's latest. "Going once, going—"

Lauryn raised her bidding paddle, her eyes on Gavin, who stood beside the auctioneer. "Ten thousand."

A startled gasp from the crowd told her no one was topping the bid. But all the while, she didn't shift her attention from Gavin.

The man who'd promised he'd never leave her if she gave him another chance. She hoped he could see what her gesture meant, even if she'd been bidding with his money. She wanted to give them both a second chance.

"Going once, going twice, sold to bidder number twenty-nine!" the auctioneer called before moving on to the evening's final bachelors.

Vaguely, Lauryn felt her friends' hugs and heard their congratulations before she made her way toward the back of the room near the steps to the stage. Angling through the crowd, words of congratulations and even a bit of teasing echoing around her with every step closer. Finally, she reached the golden rope and moved it aside to claim her prize. Claim her man.

Gavin was already waiting for her, his arms out-stretched.

Lauryn stepped into them, holding him tight. Breathing in the cedar scent of his aftershave as she tucked her head against his chest. The rest of the arena faded as they stood in the shadows of the fundraiser.

They held one another for a long moment before Gavin edged back to look into her eyes. "I'm so sorry for not seeing everything I had in front of me. I've been so busy being hurt and angry with my father that I didn't see the hurt I was causing my brothers. To you."

His hand cradled her face as he tipped it up to his.

She melted at the contact, appreciating his words even if they weren't necessary any longer. She had seen the truth of them in his eyes when he'd walked out onto that stage earlier. He carried pain and baggage from the past just as she did. But they hadn't let it break them.

And she wasn't going to let it steal their future. "I

was hasty and on edge, all too willing to take offense because I was—"

"You were entitled to being on edge." He cupped her shoulders, fingers massaging lightly. "It was the worst-possible day for you."

She shook her head, her heart aching with how close she'd come to ruining things with him forever. "No. The worst-possible day for me is the one where I lose you."

If she'd had any doubts about how he felt about her, they evaporated now as his shoulders slumped with relief. She hadn't realized how tense he'd still been until that moment.

"Lauryn, I love you, more than I can express. But I want to have the time to find the words to explain how precious you are to me." His hands rubbed up and down her arms, as if he could rub the truth of them into the skin bared by her halter-top dress. "And I'm willing to do whatever it takes to make things work between us. To make things as happy and beautiful as you deserve."

Her heart fluttered. She shivered with the feelings his touch stirred. Awareness, and so much more.

"Then let's start now," she urged, remembering well that forever wasn't always guaranteed. With Gavin at her side, she wanted to keep living her dreams, working to make them come true every single day. "Let's begin our future tonight. I love you, too, and I don't want to wait another day to begin the happiness we *both* deserve."

Gavin wrapped his arms around her again, pulling her against his chest and holding her tight against his crisp lapel. "I don't know how I got so lucky, but I'm not going to question it. I'm just going to make sure you never regret choosing me."

Feeling her first and best dream already coming true, Lauryn kissed him with all the love in her heart, taking her sweet time to do it right. Thoroughly.

Lucky for her, they had forever.

* * * * *

*Look for the next Kingsland Ranch story,
coming Spring 2023.*

*And if you liked these Western romances
from Joanne Rock, don't miss the
Return to Catamount trilogy!*

Available now!

Rocky Mountain Rivals
One Colorado Night
A Colorado Claim

#2929 DESIGNS ON A RANCHER

Texas Cattleman's Club: The Wedding • by LaQuette

When big-city designer Keely Tucker is stranded with Jacob Chatman, the sexiest, most ambitious rancher in Texas, unbridled passion ignites. But will her own Hollywood career dreams be left in the rubble?

#2930 BREAKAWAY COWBOY

High Country Hawkes • by Barbara Dunlop

Rodeo cowboy Dallas Hawkes has an injured shoulder and a suspicious nature. Giving heartbroken Sierra Armstrong refuge at his ranch is a nonstarter. But the massage therapist's touch can help heal his damaged body. And open a world of burning desire in his lonely bed...

#2931 FRIENDS...WITH CONSEQUECES

Business and Babies • by Jules Bennett

The not-so-innocent night CEO Zane Westbrook spent with his brother's best friend, Nora Monroe, was supposed to remain a secret. But their temporary fling turns permanent when she reveals she's expecting Zane's baby!

#2932 AFTER THE LIGHTS GO DOWN

by Donna Hill

It's lights, camera, *scandal* when competing morning-show news anchors Layne Davis and Paul Waverly set their sights on their next career goals. Especially as their ambitions and attraction collide on set...and seductive sparks explode behind closed doors!

#2933 ONE NIGHT WAGER

The Gilbert Curse • by Katherine Garbera

When feisty small-town Indy Belmont takes on bad boy celebrity chef Conrad Gilbert in a local cook-off, neither expects a red-hot attraction. Winning a weekend in his strong, sexy arms may be prize enough! But only if Indy can tame her headstrong beast...

#2934 BIG EASY SECRET

Bad Billionaires • by Kira Sinclair

Jameson Neally and Kinley Sullivan are two of the best computer hackers in the world. Cracking code is easy. But cracking the walls around their guarded hearts? Impossible! When the two team up on a steamy game of cat and mouse, will they catch their culprit...or each other?

Get 4 FREE REWARDS!

We'll send you 2 FREE Books <u>plus</u> 2 FREE Mystery Gifts.

FREE Value Over $20

Both the **Harlequin® Desire** and **Harlequin Presents®** series feature compelling novels filled with passion, sensuality and intriguing scandals.

YES! Please send me 2 FREE novels from the Harlequin Desire or Harlequin Presents series and my 2 FREE gifts (gifts are worth about $10 retail). After receiving them, if I don't wish to receive any more books, I can return the shipping statement marked "cancel." If I don't cancel, I will receive 6 brand-new Harlequin Presents Larger-Print books every month and be billed just $6.30 each in the U.S. or $6.49 each in Canada, a savings of at least 10% off the cover price, or 6 Harlequin Desire books every month and be billed just $5.05 each in the U.S. or $5.74 each in Canada, a savings of at least 12% off the cover price. It's quite a bargain! Shipping and handling is just 50¢ per book in the U.S. and $1.25 per book in Canada.* I understand that accepting the 2 free books and gifts places me under no obligation to buy anything. I can always return a shipment and cancel at any time by calling the number below. The free books and gifts are mine to keep no matter what I decide.

Choose one: ☐ **Harlequin Desire**
(225/326 HDN GRJ7)

☐ **Harlequin Presents Larger-Print**
(176/376 HDN GRJ7)

Name (please print)

Address   Apt. #

City   State/Province   Zip/Postal Code

Email: Please check this box ☐ if you would like to receive newsletters and promotional emails from Harlequin Enterprises ULC and its affiliates. You can unsubscribe anytime.

Mail to the Harlequin Reader Service:
IN U.S.A.: P.O. Box 1341, Buffalo, NY 14240-8531
IN CANADA: P.O. Box 603, Fort Erie, Ontario L2A 5X3

Want to try 2 free books from another series? Call 1-800-873-8635 or visit www.ReaderService.com.

---

*Terms and prices subject to change without notice. Prices do not include sales taxes, which will be charged (if applicable) based on your state or country of residence. Canadian residents will be charged applicable taxes. Offer not valid in Quebec. This offer is limited to one order per household. Books received may not be as shown. Not valid for current subscribers to the Harlequin Presents or Harlequin Desire series. All orders subject to approval. Credit or debit balances in a customer's account(s) may be offset by any other outstanding balance owed by or to the customer. Please allow 4 to 6 weeks for delivery. Offer available while quantities last.

Your Privacy—Your information is being collected by Harlequin Enterprises ULC, operating as Harlequin Reader Service. For a complete summary of the information we collect, how we use this information and to whom it is disclosed, please visit our privacy notice located at corporate.harlequin.com/privacy-notice. From time to time we may also exchange your personal information with reputable third parties. If you wish to opt out of this sharing of your personal information, please visit readerservice.com/consumerschoice or call 1-800-873-8635. **Notice to California Residents**—Under California law, you have specific rights to control and access your data. For more information on these rights and how to exercise them, visit corporate.harlequin.com/california-privacy.

HDHP22R3

HARLEQUIN
PLUS

Announcing a **BRAND-NEW** multimedia subscription service for romance fans like you!

Read, Watch and Play.

Experience the easiest way to get the romance content you crave.

Start your **FREE 7 DAY TRIAL** at <u>www.harlequinplus.com/freetrial</u>.